© MÉLANIE MORAND

DONALD ANTRIM is a regular contributor to *The New Yorker* and has received fellowships from the National Endowment for the Arts, the John Simon Guggenheim Memorial Foundation, and the New York Public Library. He lives in New York City.

ALSO BY **DONALD ANTRIM**

The Afterlife: A Memoir
The Verificationist
The Hundred Brothers

ADDITIONAL PRAISE FOR

ELECT MR. ROBINSON FOR A BETTER WORLD

"*Elect Mr. Robinson for a Better World* is an audaciously imagined work of whimsy and wonder." —*Salon*

"Donald Antrim is hardly the first novelist to investigate the psychosexual chaos roaring behind the orderly affluence of middle-class life, but he may be the most imaginative." —*Chicago Sun-Times*

"How do you describe the offbeat novels of Donald Antrim? How about edgy, fantastical, absurdist, Dionysian, visionary." —*Newsday*

"A superbly entertaining and mischievously imagined first novel . . . Arresting . . . Antrim is a wonderful, truly original comic writer." —*St. Petersburg Times* (Florida)

"A breezy, darkly comic lampoon of civic duty and ambition . . . Antrim's crisp, effective prose and Robinson's odd academic notions echo Don DeLillo's *White Noise*. There is much to chuckle at, and even a bit to ponder in this imaginative debut." —*Publishers Weekly*

"Pete, though mad as a hatter, comments on the grisly goings-on (including his ritual burial of the ex-mayor's body parts) with a cool, ironic intelligence. . . . Antrim is a promising new talent with a wonderfully keen ear." —*Kirkus Reviews*

ELECT MR. ROBINSON
FOR A BETTER WORLD

DONALD **ANTRIM**

ELECT MR. ROBINSON
FOR A BETTER WORLD

WITH A NEW INTRODUCTION BY
JEFFREY EUGENIDES

PICADOR

FARRAR, STRAUS AND GIROUX
NEW YORK

 Printed in the United States of America. For information, address Picador, 175 Fifth Avenue, New York, N.Y. 10010.

www.picadorusa.com
www.twitter.com/picadorusa • www.facebook.com/picadorusa

Picador® is a U.S. registered trademark and is used by Farrar, Straus and Giroux under license from Pan Books Limited.

For book club information, please visit www.facebook.com/picadorbookclub or e-mail marketing@picadorusa.com.

Portions of this novel originally appeared in *Harper's* magazine and *The Paris Review.*

ISBN 978-0-312-66210-3 (trade paperback)
ISBN 978-1-4299-7737-1 (e-book)

First published in the United States by Viking Penguin, a division of Penguin Putnam Inc.

First Picador Edition: June 2012

10 9 8 7 6 5 4 3 2 1

FOR DON AND ROXANNE SELF

INTRODUCTION BY
JEFFREY EUGENIDES

THE BARBARITY OF THE PRESENT

One bright New York day over two decades ago—1990 or thereabouts—in a booth at the Viand Diner, on Second Avenue and Eighty-sixth Street, Donald Antrim handed me the first twenty pages of a manuscript that became, in the fullness of time, *Elect Mr. Robinson for a Better World.* This was back in the waning days of the typewriter, Antrim's model, if I remember correctly, being a slim Olivetti whose keystrokes left impressions on those onion-skin sheets as delicate, airy, and stylish as the opening lines: "See a town stucco-pink, fishbelly-white, done up in wisteria and swaying palms and smelling of rotted fruits broken beneath trees: mango, papaya, delicious tangerine; imagine the town rising from coral shoals bleached and cutting upward through bathwater seas: the sunken world of fish. That's what my wife, Meredith, calls the ocean." At the time, I didn't know that this paragraph commenced not only the manuscript I was holding but two others that would follow, comprising what came to be a trilogy of short novels narrated by pedantic, syntactically well-behaved, semi-insane middle-aged men. I had no idea that marine imagery would play such a large role in the novel (later on, Meredith's self-induced "ichthyomorphic trances" become a barrier in her marriage to the narrator). All I knew was that, following the trajectory of those opening lines, I was suddenly pulled into a never-before-experienced realm: the sunken world of a strange and marvelous book. *Elect Mr. Robinson for a Better World* is that very rare thing: a book without antecedents. To compare it to other books is to invite frustration: the templates don't match up. The novel is satirical without becoming satire. It presents recognizable characters in a recognizably American suburb without conforming to realism. It projects psychological disturbance onto the external world without indulging in the gothic. It is a work of the utmost originality and artistic courage and it gets better, and deeper, each time you read it.

The narrator of the novel is Pete Robinson, an unemployed schoolteacher and medieval history buff. As the book opens, Pete is up in his "padlocked attic," observing his hometown through binoculars. Things don't look so good. The schools have closed. The ex-mayor, Jim Kunkel, has recently been drawn and quartered in retribution for his having lobbed Stinger missiles into the Botanical Garden reflecting pool, killing former constituents. In addition, town residents have dug spike-embedded "pits" outside their houses to protect themselves from neighbors. Two families are engaging in small-scale warfare in a city park. Meanwhile, "[e]verything, houses and stores, gas stations and banks, all the landmarks of my happy life in this place I love—everything seems to be sinking. How sad things seem then. I half expect to see reptiles emerging openmouthed from bay windows, snakes dripping from aluminum mailboxes and low gratings overhanging two-car garages. It's a scene from dreams, a watery place familiar but not familiar, home but not home, dredged from within and carrying up intimations of loss, of desire, of my increasingly intense premonition of death by drowning."

Pete describes the local disarray in the methodical voice of the "Town Scrivener" he happens to be. A running gag in the book involves Pete's preoccupation with drawing up "lecture notes" in his attic redoubt. (He calls these notes "work God gave [him] to do.") As readers, we never get to see these notes; what we get, instead, is this book, Pete's account not only of how wrong things have gone but, more significantly, of what he plans to do to rectify them. Reviewing the events leading up to the mayor's execution, Pete says: "I'd given a talk, only days before, on an array of such devices, at a Rotary lunch. My intention was to draw parallels between ancient and modern concepts of punishment and guilt, and to demonstrate a few ways contemporary society has internalized, even institutionalized 'The Barbarity of the Past,' which was the title of my talk." Pete's motives, as he understands them, are commendable; he wishes to enlighten, to instruct. But something always gets in the way. His lecture, for instance, serves only to get him nicknamed "Mr. Executioner" by the townsmen who seek his assistance in killing the ex-mayor, a request Pete, to his later regret, readily complies with, going so far as to suggest that they use "Toyotas and Subarus, in lieu of horses." In a dying request, Jim Kunkel asks Pete to dismember his body and scatter its pieces in the manner of Osiris. Pete promises to do this, but instead stores Kunkel's internal organs in his freezer, managing to bury only a foot, which bleeds onto some fig bars another character mistakenly eats.

Yet, for all this, Pete isn't deterred. His wanderings through the blighted landscape are accompanied by thoughts of resurrection and renewal. He wants to run for mayor. He toys with campaign slogans: PETE ROBINSON FOR PEACE ON EARTH. PETE ROBINSON, A STEP TOWARD PARADISE. The title of the novel is itself a campaign slogan, and much of Pete's verbiage has the ring of political rhetoric. He's constantly explaining, theorizing, bringing history and cultural lore to bear on the immediate situation. Pete knows a lot of stuff—about *The Egyptian Book of the Dead,* Portuguese torture chambers, elementary school pedagogy—but nothing that he knows helps him understand his world. The sense that knowledge itself—history, the Western canon, you name it—is falling into ruin just as surely as the town pervades the novel, and since this, too, is a book, something of that decay gets imparted on your hands as you read.

Pete's dreams of becoming mayor, like his hopes of opening a school in his home, exist in opposition to the decadence of the municipal, political, and educational systems. The taxpayers have defunded the schools. The former schoolhouse has been turned into a factory for the manufacture of talismans made from coral. Pete's wife, Meredith, gives him one of these trinkets, signifying her membership in the growing fish cults. This seaside Florida town, in an unspecified location, in an unspecified year, has receded into a primitive condition where superstitions flourish and citizens understand themselves to be inhabited by invisible forces. The book's narrative strategy perfectly suits this, for Pete's own loquacity, his veneer of rationality, is a shell for dark forces within. Just why is he so interested in the Inquisition, anyway? Why, in his basement, is Pete building a "1:32-scale, exhibition-quality balsa-and-Styrofoam cutaway reproduction of a Portuguese interrogation chamber (circa 1600), complete with rack, miniature shackles fashioned from spray-painted costume-jewelry chokers and clasps, and Q-tips representing albino rats"? Though Pete considers himself the possible savior of the town, the fact that he wants to be mayor links him to the former officeholder, the deadly Kunkel. What mayoral duties does Pete, in his heart of hearts, want to assume? Who is he really?

Since the publication of *Elect Mr. Robinson,* dystopic fiction has become something of a fad. Antrim was there early, if not first. Certainly today, in the wake of 9/11 and the appearance of border militias, right-to-carry laws, and survivalist bunkers, this novel seems even more prescient than it did when it came out in 1993. But "dystopic" describes neither the madness nor the method here. The heart of Antrim's enterprise, the thing that allows him to make credible his wild surmises, is his keen insight into social and marital relations and his masterful linguistic skills. Antrim sketches his characters—Rotarians, tennis buffs, suburban moms, wayward teens—with indelible lines. They speak a perfectly rendered American argot. They go about their lives doing all the things comfortably domesticized Americans do. They attend potluck suppers, ogle one another's spouses, chauffeur children to appointments, borrow plumber's snakes, all in pursuit of happiness in a place where happiness can no longer exist. "The Clam Castle was crowded with taxpayers," Pete says in typical fashion. "Jerry, Bill, Abe, Tom, Robert, Betsy, Dick, and many other business professionals including several of my old teaching colleagues: Alan, Simone, Doug; and all the spouses, too, along with a few children old enough to be trusted to stay quiet during open discussion; and Meredith's mother, Helen, who hated the status quo and was apt to be vociferous; and, of course, Terry, whose generous all-you-can-eat-for-one-special-low-price deal was the reason we were convened at the Clam Castle in the first place." The amount of information Antrim manages to pack into this sentence is amazing. First, we get Pete's insufferable predilection for the comprehensive, as he reels off a genealogy worthy of Homer's *Iliad;* next, we glean his secret misgivings about children (Pete and Meredith are childless) as well as his feelings about his mother-in-law; we get the blandness of contemporary speech ("business professionals") as well as specifics about the participants' ongoing interest, despite the town's much larger problems, in economizing by eating fast food, a touch that ends the sentence on a note of high humor and reinforces the suburban realism. The verisimilitude enhances the novel's surreality rather than detracting from it. In Antrim's hands, scenes of elaborate fancy give birth to moments as emotionally telling as those in Chekhov. For instance, when Meredith "becomes" a coelacanth, cavorting with other coelacanths in the sea, Pete asks her, "Can I become one, can I come with you?" Meredith's hilarious answer is also heartbreaking: "That's the thing, Pete, you have to be there already, and you weren't. I'm sorry, honey." What better metaphor to describe the estrangement within marriage and the impermanence of love? This dual or triple register represents the chief characteristic of this unclassifiable book, and of Antrim's fiction in general. Lots of writers can be, by turns, sad, funny, frightening, or ludicrous. Antrim does all these things *at once.* He infuses multiple shades of meaning into singular scenes, even sentences. This is why *Elect Mr. Robinson* is so hard to interpret. The emotional cues aren't those we recognize from reading other novels. They happen here, and only here.

For a slim book, written with some of the most beautiful, scrupulously punctuated, well-modulated prose you'll ever read, *Elect Mr. Robinson for a Better World* is also one of the most violent. The violence isn't ritualistic or softened by comic excess, as it is in the other two books of the trilogy, *The Hundred Brothers* and *The Verificationist.* Here, it erupts unexpectedly, corrosively. I can hardly think of another novel that turns the table on the reader so completely. For much of the book, you're either smiling or laughing out loud, but as the story proceeds, and abruptly in its last pages (as we learn why Pete is locked in the attic), a chill sets in. Against all odds, this very funny novel becomes truly scary, and as though blundering into Pete's own camouflaged pit, the reader falls onto the sharpened stakes of the book's terrifying ending.

The dead ex-mayor comes as close as any character to naming what ails the little palm-shrouded town. At that same Rotary luncheon where Pete delivers his talk, Kunkel stands up to announce, "We're all murderers here," a piece of truth-telling that outrages his neighbors and leads, in no small part, to his demise. *Elect Mr. Robinson for a Better World* makes a similar charge, attesting to the barbarity not of the past but of the present, and the response from the reader, especially the American reader, is likely to be just as uncomfortable, angry, and full of guilty recognition. In a reversal of Marx's famous line about history in *The 18th Brumaire,* the major events in this novel occur first as farce and *then* as tragedy. Kunkel's death scene, though creepy, is played mostly for laughs. His calling everyone a murderer is similarly charged with humor. But by the book's end we realize the dread seriousness of the mayor's words. It's as if Antrim has wrung out every bit of comedy from the texture of his tale, leaving a poisonous residue.

Of course, the novel does much more than castigate. It is, after all, a work of literature, and provides a more classical catharsis than might be expected from a novel with considerable experimental qualities. Despite his oddness, we like Pete. In this altered world, he is our only guide. You can't help wishing that Meredith would come back to him. You hope things go well for him on the first day of school. When they don't, and when Pete's true character is revealed, the reader experiences emotions every bit as intense and purgative as Aristotelian poetics stipulate: terror at what Pete does and pity for his victim, poor "little auburn-haired Sarah Miller." You finish this book hollowed out, stunned by the lengths to which Antrim has gone to make real and palpable, in a piece of unrealistic fiction, the nature of evil. In addition, the reader's sympathy with Pete, won little by little throughout the course of the book in such a light-fingered fashion that you might not even notice it, serves as a form of self-incrimination. Pete's unawareness of the dark forces inside him has the effect of making the reader wonder how much this might be true of everyone. Finishing the book, therefore, you feel terror at, and pity for, your own self.

Despite its lugubrious subject matter and its acerbic estimate of human nature, this novel is the opposite of destructive, however. In its humor and deep sadness, and especially in the rigor of its prose and the intelligent flow of Pete's thoughts, however loopy, *Elect Mr. Robinson for a Better World* delights as well as lacerates. With genuine artfulness Donald Antrim enacts something of the resurgence that Pete hopes to do by burying Jim Kunkel's foot. "Indeed," Pete writes, "it was as if it were not Jim Kunkel's foot being buried, not Jim's foot at all, but a flesh-and-blood vessel containing the Hopes of Men—Jim, me, anybody and everybody—for a better, wiser world that might spring from soil made fertile by blood and bone." Despite the arch tone of that sentence, it nicely describes both Antrim's intention and achievement. This necrotic book buries itself deep in your brain, and despite its purulent content, gives life.

ELECT MR. ROBINSON

FOR A BETTER WORLD

SEE A TOWN stucco-pink, fishbelly-white, done up in wisteria and swaying palms and smelling of rotted fruits broken beneath trees: mango, papaya, delicious tangerine; imagine this town rising from coral shoals bleached and cutting upward through bathwater seas: the sunken world of fish. That's what my wife, Meredith, calls the ocean. Her father was an oysterman. Of course, that trade's dead now, like so many that once sustained this paradise. Looking from my storm window, I can see Meredith's people scavenging the shoreline. Down they bend, troweling wet dunes with plastic toy shovels: yellow, red, blue. The yellow one, I know, belongs to Meredith's mother. I want to call to Helen, to wave and exchange greetings, but I know she'll never acknowledge me after the awful things that happened to little auburn-haired Sarah Miller, early last week, down in my basement.

Tragic.

The diggers make their shabby way up the coastline. Who would've imagined a subsistence industry erected around the magical properties of dead sea creatures? But it's true. Look inland. There's the converted elementary school with wall clocks endlessly proclaiming three o'clock. It's a factory now. They're in there, day and night, making starfish fetishes and totems of cowry, sea cucumber, washed-up wood. I can hear crunching routers shaping precious black coral into the rings and charms everyone around here wears, and I hear the lawn-mower growl of a dozen diesels parked outside the school and giving extra electricity through high-voltage cables blackly snaked beneath the jungle gym, across the basketball black-top, around the chain-link fence wrapping the tennis courts.

At center court, a woman wearing whites lofts a ball; it captures day's brilliant light glancing off the hurricane flood-control canals along South Main—the intercoastal grid: deep, long arms of gator-plagued water crisscrossing landfill. The woman's racket cannonades the ball into the opposing court. It sails, bounces. There's no one there, just balls. The woman owns a children's clothing store on Pettigrew. I hoist my bin-oculars and close-focus on grit streaking her mirror-tinted sunglasses, on clay dust rising in explosive mushrooms around her shuffling feet. And there are gray smudges on her box-pleated tennis skirt, clay scuffed from the playing surface by impacting tennis balls, sweatily transferred to her hand, wiped absently, wetly away in the radiant summer heat ushering ozone's traces sweetly beneath advancing clouds.

Afternoon rain, here it comes out of the west. The woman serves, the rain approaches; and now the school cafeteria door—newly painted a rich midnight blue, which may or may not be significant—opens; a man peers up and out at the coming wall of water. I can see his heavy face. He's Ray Conover, whose wife, Miriam, died so horribly when Jim Kunkel made that sorry, stupid show of indiscriminately lob-bing Stinger missiles into the Botanical Garden reflecting pool. Many picnickers died that day. I recall Ray walking up

Main, oblivious to traffic, blood-soaked and carrying his wife's corpse.

This was at summer's end, only a short while ago, right around the time school should've begun but didn't because, of course, we lost the schools when the taxpayers elected to defund the system.

It was a black hour. We got together—the board members and teaching faculty still on payroll and fit to head class—and decided to hold school out of our own pockets if necessary, but were subsequently unable to settle on a suitable physical plant for pre-, lower-, and middle-school sections. It wasn't that we needed lots of space. We didn't. We had only a handful of kids, and could reasonably have adopted a Little Red Schoolhouse approach. But all of us, Meredith, myself, Doug, Marty, Allan, Simone, everybody—we all believed in the compartmentalization of study topics and the enhancement of student self-esteem through upward, graded progression. Bio one year, chem the next. We didn't want to let go of that. So we insisted on grade-designated classrooms with separate sections for electives, even though we knew certain courses would have only two or three enrollees, or one, or none.

We were afraid. We were overwrought.

Today, sitting here in my padlocked attic, with a heap of class notes to prepare and these "Extra Wide Angle" precision-optical field glasses to spy around with—today I'm not sure I'd favor drawing and quartering an ex-mayor and Chamber of Commerce volunteer. That's what we did to Jim Kunkel after the Stinger incident. For my part, let me say, right here and now, I'm sorry for the role I played in the kangaroo court that assembled outside Jim's Dune Road condominium.

Then again, what could I do? The demands of civic discourse are difficult. Cooperation and conviviality are rewarded in many ways. I wanted a schoolhouse. I was thinking of the kids when Jerry Henderson and Bill Nixon and some other Rotary guys greeted me beneath the streetlamps. They well knew my journeyman-historian's acquaintance with the rack, the wheel, the iron maiden, and so forth. I'd given a talk, only days before, on an array of such devices, at a Rotary lunch. My intention was to draw parallels between ancient and modern concepts of punishment and guilt, and to demonstrate a few of the ways contemporary society has internalized, even subtly institutionalized "The Barbarity of the Past," which was the title of my talk.

I was hoping to say something about the way we live. It was clear to me, though, during the question-and-answer period, that the real effect of my lecture had been pernicious. Should I have seen it coming, that starry night outside Jim's Dune Road home, when Jerry and Bill and those bully boys clapped their hands on my back and said, grinning, "Hey, it's Mr. Executioner"?

Likewise, how much responsibility must I bear for what eventually, inevitably occurred, simply because I suggested using some Toyotas and Subarus parked nearby, in lieu of horses?

Better, perhaps, not to ask. Anyway, I have lecture notes to prepare. It's what I'm supposed to be doing, it's work God gave me to do, instead of gazing out my window at the clothing store owner's radiant brown body. How morbid, this voyeurism of mine. It's a sickness: low-grade agoraphobia merged with a troubling fixation on rain running from tile roofs into curbside gutters clogged with rotting vegetation.

They back up, the gutters, choking muck. The skies blacken, moisture descends, canals rise, lawns puddle, the unswept streets slowly fill. Everything, houses and stores, gas stations and banks, all the landmarks of my happy life in this place I love—everything seems to be sinking. How sad things seem then. I half expect to see reptiles emerging openmouthed from bay windows, snakes dripping from aluminum mailboxes and low gratings overhanging two-car garages. It's a scene from dreams, a watery place familiar but not familiar, home but not home, dredged from within and carrying up intimations of loss, of desire, of my increasingly intense premonition of death by drowning.

It remains to be seen if today's showers will fall hard enough, or last long enough, to have this effect of transforming the world.

Here's something to indicate a grim forecast: Ray Conover, slouching among the diesels ganged and snarling outside the ex-school—*my* ex-school—walls, shutting down motors, making the day quiet enough to hear a distant bell buoy irregularly pealing from seas that are surely rising. And from closer, the echoes of tennis balls solidly struck. I'd not, until now, noticed the sound of these collisions. The woman's racket arcs upward toward a furry ball traveling its vertical course to the apex of stillness. The hit is made, the ball rockets. An incalculable instant later, I hear *whomp.*

Does she realize she's on the verge of getting drenched? Maybe from behind her silver, locust-eye lenses, the world looks weatherless.

Ray fiddles with a diesel machine. He doesn't look well to me. His trousers are too short and his shirt is torn. Rangy beard creeps down his neck. He might be an overweight, sunburned wino, loafing away the day. Ray Conover, however, is no bum; he's a widely published statistical oceanographer specializing in subtropical coastal ecosystems. I assume he's at the old school in a consulting capacity and that he's only out in the yard performing menial engine-maintenance tasks as a favor to someone inside. Or as an excuse to escape the relentless crunching and grinding going on in there. It must hurt him to watch his beloved reef get pounded to trinkets.

I have a trinket from the reef. It's a ring of polished black coral, nice-looking actually, clean and simple and altogether elegant, though sizes too large for any of my fingers. It's a gift from Meredith—otherwise I'd probably've jettisoned it by now. I don't believe in talismans, and frankly I find the water and fish cults growing up around here more than a little irksome. For example? When I jokingly remarked to Meredith that the ring might serve as a sexual device, she said, "Please don't blaspheme, okay?"

We'd just finished dinner. It was a weeknight. It seemed tiresome to point out the fact that blasphemy implies faith. At any rate, my wife's gift, in its miniature custom box lined in indigo velvet and lidded in coarse plasticine material resembling a horseshoe crab's exoskeleton, came as a surprise. She said, "You don't have to be sarcastic, Pete. It's just a little present. That's all it is."

"Thank you, hon."

"It's black coral."

"Really?"

"It'll protect you."

I replaced it in its case, then cleared the dinner dishes,

making sure to empty the fish bones into the disposal, where Meredith couldn't get at them in order to self-induce another of her ichthyomorphic trances.

But back to the Kunkel business. I can't get it out of my mind. I keep seeing Jim's face, lit red by taillights, in the long moments before the lines snapped taut, while Bill Nixon tried and retried to start his fume-spewing, out-of-tune Celica. It was all so profoundly uncomfortable; there was nothing to do but toe the grass and stare up at the stars in the sky, and listen to that revving and choking, and, of course, to Jim Kunkel, trussed, bound, spread out and spread-eagle on his belly, weeping. Heavy nylon test, the kind sport fishermen around here use to haul in tarpon, radiated from Jim's wrists and ankles, ran across grass and Jim's beautiful Japanese rock garden to the back bumpers of cars poised to travel different directions. I wanted to tell Jim it would be over quickly, that it wouldn't hurt. In fact I suspected otherwise. I was particularly concerned over the use of fishing line for a heavy-stress operation like this. Leaders might hold, or snap, in any of a wide range of infuriating combinations. Success depended on a clean, even pull, with no lurching—just like hauling aboard a big fish.

After a while it became clear that Nixon's engine was flooding; and, as well, the battery was at risk, grinding down, so Jerry Henderson wisely suggested, "Bill, give it a rest." The other guys turned off their motors too. It was agreed to wait five minutes, then try again. By the shrubs, in the driveway, at road's edge, men huddled: Jerry and Bill, Dick Morton, Abraham de Leon, Tom Thompson, Terry Heinemann, Robert Isaac. Did they hear Jim's sobbing? It occurred to me to go to Jim and rest my hand on his shoulder, to hold him or wipe his forehead, possibly scratch an itch if he felt one. That seemed right. Yes. And to apologize: for the sentence, for the delay in carrying it out, for whatever.

"Pete," Jim whispered, as if prescient.

"Jim?" I glanced around at the other men. Had they heard Jim call my name? Would talking to the condemned man affect my status among them? But no. No one seemed to notice me edging discreetly toward the ex-mayor. No one seemed to see my body haloed in dim light spilling yellowly from Jim's bug-deterrent porch bulb.

"An angel, I'm in heaven," Jim said.

"It's me, Jim. Pete." I came close to him. I could've reached down and touched him.

"My friend," he said, shaking his outstretched hands to indicate the lines knotted there. "They're cutting me."

What use describing the necessity of secure bonds, the mechanics of tugging as opposed to jerking? "Sorry," I told him. I noticed a growing crowd murmuring beyond the lawn perimeter. Spectators. Jim said, "You know, Pete, I was on the hiring committee that reviewed your application to teach third grade. How long ago was that?"

"Years."

"Ours was a mayor's office screening procedure, mind you, no actual decision authority. Purely advisory. We went over your résumé very carefully. *Very* carefully. What do you think we advised?"

"I don't know."

"What do you suppose the mayor's office told the school board about young Pete Robinson?"

"I don't know, Jim."

"Guess." His neck muscles visibly strained, his head craned upward; and his hands still lightly waved—the impression was of some neurologic episode. He complained, "You're not a lot of fun, are you? Won't even guess."

I figured he was probably in shock. But he spoke again, saying, "You got the job, right? Think about it." So I did, I thought about it. And realized, or thought I realized, thinking about it, what this was all about, why we were out here doing what we were doing, why Jim's death had to happen. Jim was no ordinary citizen. He'd once been mayor. He'd held influence over my life, over all our lives.

Now he would suffer a death consequent of dire actions, appropriate to high station: an old leader turned rogue, sundered by the people.

I knelt down close to Jim's liver-spotted head and whispered to him, "You knew this would happen, didn't you, old man? You did it for us. Sacrificing those families at the Botanical Garden. You knew your blood would be glue to hold this community together."

"You're crazy," he sputtered as, from another part of the lawn, Jerry Henderson's voice announced, "Gentlemen, it is time." Car doors slammed. Tears blended with saliva at the corners of Jim's mouth as, one by one, the automobiles' engines did ignite—all except the Celica's.

"Fuck," Bill Nixon said.

From the crowd came a cry: "Jumper cables! Who's got jumper cables?"

A minute later Abraham de Leon's blue Dodge van advanced alongside Kunkel's budding white hydrangeas. "Come on, Abe," coaxed Jerry Henderson as the van growled past Jim's driftwood mailbox and into the drive and toward him, toward Henderson, spotlit, now, in high-beam van light, waving his arms flight deck style, pointing a clear route to the stalled vehicle. I couldn't help noticing how Abraham's Dodge's headlights threw Jerry Henderson's shadow massively onto Jim's oversized garage door: as Abraham approached, Jerry's shadow, methodically, cryptically gesturing, grew; it loomed over us like an animate, pharaonic wall frieze.

I asked Jim, "Hey, do you know anything about Egyptian religion?"

"No. And Pete, could you please loosen these knots? I mean, if this is going to take all night?"

I watched Jerry, Bill, and Abraham fiddling with cables and plugs. I saw Tom Thompson leaning on his parked Mazda. I saw men I knew mixing with others I didn't, all muttering to one another or looking away, as though no hogtied person lay at the center of this green place. It was as if boundaries had been painted. No one outside seemed willing to acknowledge the interior space or its contents—me and Jim—and it seemed to me, then, that this might be characteristic of what some call holy ground, and that the boundary was drawn of shame. With this in mind I said to Jim, "It's not for me to loosen your bonds," and began telling about Osiris King of Kings, son of Earth and Sky, who was deceived into entering his own coffin, which drifted down the Nile and was delivered to Set, King of the Underworld; and about how the corpse was cut into pieces; and how the pieces were scattered east, west, north, south, across the land; a hand here, a foot there, buried in holy graves.

"That's beautiful," Jim said.

Over by the umbilically linked cars, Jerry counseled, "Try her again." Abraham de Leon juiced his V-8 to a high-RPM whine. Bill Nixon's Celica clattered, spit, and caught. "All right!" Abe cheered, tastelessly, as he backed the van into the hydrangeas. Jerry lowered the Celica's hood, then called out to all the drivers waiting like impatient race contestants, "Let's do this thing!"

It was my cue to back off. Everywhere, people melted away from the center, even those already standing thirty, forty feet distant. "Get away from there," mothers called to children. No one knew what this event might possibly involve in the way of spectator risk, so everybody got out of the yard, beyond cars, mailboxes, streetlight posts, citrus trees, deep into night's shadow across Dune Road. Everybody but me. I was listening to Jim's last words:

"Will you do a favor for me, Pete? After I'm gone?"

"Sure."

"Scatter my body, and declare those places holy."

Cars strained, lines tugged. I said, "I don't know, Jim. That sounds kind of heavy."

"Please, Pete."

"Well."

"Please."

"Okay, okay. I'll do it."

But enough. What's done is done. I'm just depressing myself. It's time to buckle down and prepare class notes and lecture outlines; or maybe, for a change, do my duty as Town Scrivener and type up these dog-eared town meeting minutes with their proposals concerning funding for the library system and regular-basis voluntary mine sweeps of Turtle Pond Park and surrounding wooded areas, to locate and physically deactivate, once and for all, the hundreds of claymores placed by Ed Benson during the spirited conflict between the Bensons and the Websters, who lived across the park from each other during the time of buildup and fortification, when almost everybody seemed to have barbed wire scrolled around his or her backyard, as well as maybe a sod- or tarp-covered pit laid deep with danger.

Those pits caught on. They were the rage. Everybody just had to build one.

Abraham de Leon, for instance, dug beneath his bedroom window a very deep hole embedded with croquet wickets positioned upside down and jutting skyward.

Tom Thompson, more ambitious than Abe, covered his much bigger pit in custom-cut Astroturf that rested like a dream over deeply piled shattered beer bottles, gathered, under cover of night, from the reclamation center.

Ray Conover's reef-theme memorial ditch contained a lot of extremely sharp coral draped in fabrics scissored—a poignant touch—from his dead wife's wardrobe.

And interesting was the Isaacs', over on Lovejoy. Their pit was designed by Betsy Isaac, a local earthwork installation conceptualist interested in our culture's debasement of sex. Her nonlinear pit wound serpentine from front to side yards, and was chock-full of anatomically semicorrect Barbie and Ken dolls, shredded and pulped men's magazines, several cases of hideous punch-out dime store valentines, and about two tons of dead mackerel. All in all, a provocative work, functional yet challenging.

Best of all was Jerry Henderson's moatful of water moccasins. The moat was traversable by a narrow drawbridge cobbled from redwood decking planks. The drawbridge ran on a dining room dimmer switch extension-corded to a recommissioned garage door opener secreted in a hedge.

Simple, scary, effective. Just the result I sought one warm blue Saturday morning immediately—well, more like a week—after the Kunkel thing, when I marched out back to dig. The wind blew from the east that day, and a smell of wildflowers filled the salty ocean air. I took that sweetness as a sign that things were right in the world. Meredith was there in the yard with me, reclining in an aluminum chaise, idly carving and shaping bamboo stalks macheted, the previous day, from thickets lining a nearby canal.

"I love our old house," she said as she sheared nine-foot stalks into three-foot sections. I'd planned a four-foot-deep pit, which would present an ample three feet of open fall space above a foot-high bamboo-stalk matrix. This allowed two feet of bamboo-implant anchorage, which I imagined would be sufficient for spike stability in the soft, wet, sandy backyard mud. Meredith's naked machete caught the light of the day, lent arrows of sun to tangelo leaves dangling over our fence from the McElroys' backyard citrus microgrove. She hacked a length and said, "Those condo neighborhoods along the canal get me down. They're so anonymous, I don't know how people live in them."

"I did, once."

"You were a bachelor." She razored a stalk; I spaded earth, first excavating a pre-pit outline running the length of the fence. The topsoil's top inches were grainy but yielding beneath shallow-rooted Saint Augustine grass; it was easy work to dig the grass free and fling it into low, clumpy mounds paralleling pit's edge. Nonetheless the trench grew slowly. It was a job, this ditchdigging. The sun sat high over the roofs of neighboring houses.

Meredith gestured with her machete. "Honey, how sharp do these need to be?"

I reached out and touched a green bamboo point. "That's good."

"Glad you like it. Maybe we could coat them. What's that Amazonian tree frog? Arrow-poison frog? Hunters soak their blow darts in neurotoxins secreted from its skin."

"I think we want this to serve mainly as a deterrent, not an actual death trap."

"You're so serious. I was kidding."

Deeper ground hardened. Roots blockaded the shovel's point. Most of the roots severed under impact, but one ran thick, oak-hard; the blade clanged against it. Yet no ancient hardwood graced this yard or any of the others adjacent: the McElroys', the Carters', the Kinseys'. I said to Meredith, who was whittling now, with a paring knife, fine, devilish designs, "Hey, there was a tree here once."

"What kind?"

"Can't tell. I'll have to dig around." I could feel hamstring and back muscles working hard, arms tightening above hands gloved in canvas but sore nonetheless from unaccustomed pressing against dirt packed claylike above groundwater seeping invisibly in to puddle the deepest excavations.

"Shit."

"What?"

"Water."

She peered in. She held a handful of elaborate spears-in-progress. They were beautiful. Some, I noticed, wore curvilinear fillips at their ends. Others remained blunt but showing designs shallowly traced into their exposed domes of points, anemone shapes and dolphin, laughing. Meredith joked, "We'll put some fish in," and turned and strolled barefoot to the house. Her body as she walked away was thrilling to watch. And it wasn't long before she returned with glasses, napkins, sandwiches, a pitcher of lemonade. While ants soldiered and earthworms wiggled from clay piled high nearby, we sat on prickly grass, sucking tart ice. I took off my shoes and let the grass tickle. Meredith sat a few feet away. We faced one another. Meredith semireclined and squinted into the sun. She had red in her face. I could feel a burn too, and freckles were appearing on my arms. I leaned back and rested on my elbows and watched my wife fiddle with a blade of grass; hair fell into her face and she blew it away; Meredith's long black hair lofted in strands away from her mouth and eyes. "Want to fool around?" she said.

"Now?"

"Why not?"

"We won't get this work done."

She was wearing a sundress. Clay from my digging stained her legs. I told her, "You look good to me," and she uncrossed and stretched her legs and extended her dark naked feet to brush against mine (also extended, toward her), while, with one hand pushing away loose bamboo, clearing space, a mattress of grass, she said, "Yeah?"

She stretched out, leaning back on her elbows. She was my

sweetheart. Our feet touched and our heads were far apart, we were foot to foot. I looked down the length of my body and saw her looking back at me. White salty forms of hip and stomach showed under blue cotton open at the neck in unbuttoned folds beneath Meredith's hair cascading around her eyes. She didn't move, only seemed to float hips upward, barely, lending this impression of coming closer.

Her feet moved against the bottoms of mine. "That's nice," she said.

"Yeah." I drank melted lemony ice. The muscles in Meredith's legs contracted slightly with her toes' pushing against mine; her feet pushed and I pushed back—hard. Her knees bent and up went her legs.

"Like that," I said.

And from Meredith, her own sounds: just breathing, and her whispering, "Are you hard?"

"Uh-huh."

"Show me?" Hips rising, knees coming upward revealing the backs of Meredith's legs whitely imprinted with shapes of grass. I wriggled over, got close and lay down beside her. I touched Meredith's stomach and her shoulder and her hair. I raised her lemonade glass, slipped ice into my mouth, held it melting against tongue and teeth before passing it between my wife's teeth, into her mouth, where, sucked by her, it dissolved.

"Ah," she said into my mouth.

"Ah," I breathed back.

"Ah."

"Ah."

"Yeah."

"Yeah."
"Hmn?"
"Yeah."
"How?"
"Slow."
"Mn."
"Ah."
"Mn."
"Oh."
"Mn."
"Easy."
"Sorry."
"No. Good. Great. Just not yet."
"Sure?"
"Yes. No."
"Turn me over."
"Yeah?"
"Yeah."
"Yes?"
"Yes, yes."
"Doesn't hurt?"
"No."
"Sure?"
"Sure."
"Tell me if."
"No, no, good."
"Yeah?"
"Yeah."
"Yeah?"
"Ah, no, ouch."

"Sorry."

"Okay."

"Mmn?"

"Mmn."

"Yeah?"

"Yeah."

"Ah," I breathed.

"Ah." We embraced in the harsh afternoon light. Down the street a dog barked. I looked up, through budding tree leaves, at the windows of our house.

Later, toward evening, we finished the job of burying bamboo in patterns meant to deny trespass. The pit's wide wet bottom slopped, evening's air glowed orange; Meredith and I splashed around in loosened, disarrayed clothes, getting muddy. I said, "Look how these spikes catch the sunset."

"Yes, it's pretty."

"I like this pit."

"Me too."

"I think you did lovely work with those bamboo points."

"Thanks."

"I love the one carved like a miniature beach umbrella."

"Well, I'd already started a whole beach series, and when you mentioned the water coming into the hole from the ground, it just seemed so right."

"Yeah."

"Weird, huh?"

"Kind of."

"Like getting a phone call from somebody you were just thinking about, or suddenly thinking of someone and then running smack into that person at the store. Do you believe in synchronicity, Pete?"

"I don't know."

"A lot of things happen, Pete. Look what's happening, us digging away, which is fine because we need to, but I'd just thought, doing the designs, doing the whittling, I thought I could make things less like, you know, a pit, because actually the thing that bothers me most isn't the pit, it's the way it seems natural, all of a sudden, to have it. Last year if you told me I'd be out back fucking my husband on top of a mud pile with spikes for pillows, I'd've said, No way."

Wind buffeted citrus leaves overhead, agitated green suspended fruits. I told Meredith, "It's changing times, and we're changing with them. Besides, I liked that in the mud, it was good."

"You came a lot. Sweet. Like trees."

"Trees?"

"That's not a taste, I guess, but it's what I think of."

We went into the house and took turns showering. I said, "This is like when we first met. Remember those walks past the jetty?"

"I do. You used to say, Sweetheart, give me your cunt, and I'd say, Fuck me with your tongue."

We were in the kitchen. Meredith stood by the sink. I opened the refrigerator and peered into it, visually sorting what I saw there. "How come we don't talk like that anymore?" Meredith asked.

"Maybe we're afraid. Hey, there's soup here. Is last week's bouillabaisse still good?"

"Sure."

I brought out the soup in its Tupperware container. Meredith lowered a steamer from an overhead peg. I removed the Tupperware's green top and poured the soup, carefully, so as not to splash, from container to pot, then ignited a big rear stovetop gas jet, reduced the jet to low, and placed the pot on the burner. "Stir it," Meredith said. She handed me a wooden spoon from the spoon drawer; and she said, "It's a shame we're afraid."

"Yes."

"I don't want to be afraid."

"No."

"But I am." Fish, scallops, medium shrimp, vegetables—all these things floated up, clung to bay leaves and one another in the crimson liquid, as Meredith confessed, "I'm afraid of you, Pete."

"Me?"

She leaned against the counter. Evening enveloped us. I said, "Well," even waved aloft the wooden spoon, danced it in the air, a theatrical gesture emphasizing nothing, making me feel feeble; and, too, I felt despondent in that way that seems naturally to follow sex in the afternoon, when day's last light rides horizontally down through clouds pillowed low. Surveying the light filtering through window glass to glance off shiny pots and the stove and the enameled freezer chest—clicking on, now, to cool and preserve the right hand, left foot, heart, liver, partial left lung, adrenal glands, intact genitals, and odd other freezer-wrapped bits of ex-mayor—I felt I could empathize with Meredith's apprehension of me. Of course she was afraid. Day was passing into night, death hung in the air, our happy post-coital sadness was fragile.

"Add water to the soup," she told me.

"Water?"

"Just a trickle."

I went to the tap and rotated the knob and held a glass beneath the flow. Water coursed over my wrist and fingers, and this felt nice, so I remained a minute, getting wet and wondering if Meredith had perhaps discovered and unwrapped one of those packages of Jim Kunkel tucked in the back of the freezer beneath the restaurant-sized bag of fish sticks; and if so, *which* package; and, also, if it might now be advisable to assume the worst and come right out and address the issue, to take, as it were, the initiative. Meredith said, "Honey, be careful, the sink's filling up."

Which it was. The drain was congested, and water was rapidly rising.

"Turn off the faucet, Pete."

"Right."

"Here," she said, offering me the plunger. But I told her, "I'll deal with it after dinner."

"Will you?"

"Yes."

"Promise?"

"Yes."

"Because I refuse to leave unwashed dishes out all night for the bugs. Which reminds me. Listen, before I forget, I've thought about it and I've decided that in the future I think I can handle the fifth- and sixth-grade bio sections if we combine grades on field trips. We'll go to Peterson's Farm and collect coleoptera for specimen exhibits. Maybe I can get Dr. Peterson to let one of his bees sting him on the finger. The kids always like to see that."

It was pathetic to be talking about school, when there was no such thing anymore. Nevertheless we did it all the time. We were teachers.

"You're sure you want to collect?"

"Why not?"

"Local populations are way down. I'd say just observe. Encourage conservation. Teach respect for life."

"Ha. This from a guy who assigns Clausewitz to eight-year-olds."

"We've been over that. Teaching the history and theory of warfare is a perfectly legitimate method of demonstrating patterns of social reformation in the modern era."

"Listen to you. You sound like a politician. You should run for office."

"Maybe I will." And why not. It was hardly any secret that the present civic administration was little more than a puppet front for corrupt Rotarians like Jerry Henderson and his Better Business Bureau buddies, men with no aversion to sending a town father to his death in the deep of night on a well-trimmed lawn. Sitting there in my lamplit kitchen that smelled of fish, waiting to share a meal with my wife who may or may not have recently chanced upon those body parts lying wrapped and bagged beneath frozen food (and who therefore, lacking any explanation for the presence of wrapped and bagged body parts, may or may not have been experiencing, at that very moment, considerable anxiety regarding her husband's psychological condition—I wasn't going to press her on the matter, no way)—sitting there with these concerns and every muscle twitching from a good day's honest work, it occurred to me that the Hendersons of the world had best watch out, because one day the people of this town would rise up to reaffirm old values of education and social welfare, just as Jim Kunkel surely foresaw when he laid down his life to become a martyr before God.

And who better to carry Jim's message than the very man the ex-mayor had entrusted with his mortal remains? "You truly think you can handle the bio sections?" I asked Meredith when at last we sat before large bowls brimming with sea creatures.

"Sure."

"Okay then." Between bites I outlined a plan for a provisional school in which Meredith would indeed go right ahead and acquire those fifth- and sixth-grade bio sections; as well, she'd continue in her customary guidance-counseling and grievance-arbitration roles. Which would leave lower-grade earth and marine sciences to Doug, who was a quick study, able lecturer, and genuine whiz at Play Time. I'd been meaning for years to ask Ray Conover, whom I felt the kids would undoubtedly love despite his present post-traumatic depression (who knew, maybe it would do Ray good to be with some youngsters; after all, he and Miriam never did have any of their own), to lead a trip to Midnight Pass to gather hermit crabs. And with Simone holding down art, Marty on math, Allan coaching remedial reading, and me shouldering my usual load with an added emphasis on civics and government so that the kids could witness public machinery at the grass roots level . . . who knew, maybe we could even sponsor a municipal project, some kind of a hands-on, current affairs thing—*mayoral campaign* I was thinking but not saying—we'd have a manageable curriculum with the focus on individual attention and lots of Improvised Creative Activities, ICAs, which, as I reminded my wife, are traditionally immensely underrated as learning tools. I said, "And get this, we'll do it here in the house."

"You're crazy."

"We could get your mother to teach Home Ec."

"Oh God."

"Seriously, we've got the upstairs bedrooms, the attic study, the living room and dining nook, the porch for an art studio, the kitchen, and two bathrooms. We've got that old Tandy computer for grade storage and attendance tables. It's a compromise, it's not the best of all possible worlds, but neither is the world the best of all possible worlds, is it? The kids, Meredith, think of the kids," I said as I sat there fancying this very kitchen swarming with boys and girls Magic-Markering construction-paper political campaign poster boards that brightly commanded: VOTE FOR OUR TEACHER FOR MAYOR BECAUSE HE'S THE BEST. Meredith said, "Damn, I completely forgot, Jerry Henderson called while I was making lunch. He wants you to phone him back. Sorry, I meant to write it down. He said it's urgent. I didn't know you and Jerry were friends."

"We're not."

"He called you his good pal Pete. He told me to tell his good pal Pete he's got good news for him. Any idea what that could mean?"

"Nope."

"When you find out let me know, because I could use a little good news."

Which was my feeling exactly, when, a little later that night, while Meredith readied for bed upstairs and night deepened outside, Henderson called again to thank me personally and on behalf of the citizenry for the wonderful service I'd provided the community in our recent hour of crisis out on Dune Road. He breathed into the phone, "Pete, it was a terrific idea to wire Kunkel to those cars. Only a scholar of your caliber could've come up with that. I want you to know that everybody appreciated your expertise in this matter."

It was a good connection; Jerry sounded close. In fact Jerry did live nearby, in a sprawling Tudor eyesore at the corner of Osprey and Manatee. Sometimes, on walks at night, I would round the corner and look up to see Jerry's ostentatious tile roof above faux-granite walls like theme-park castle embattlements; and I would always think of Jerry and Rita's dead daughter, Linda.

Jerry said, "Pete, the boys have worked out an arrangement and there's a potentially high-quality educational facility available at Freedom Field, with blacktop flooring and good northern exposure if you keep the door open and don't mind the occasional flyover."

"Freedom Field? An airplane hangar?"

"Pete, she's twenty thousand square feet with forty-foot ceilings. Perfect for basketball or indoor tennis if you paint lines and string nets. Tell me, what sports do you tend to offer at the elementary level?"

"Sports? Let's see. Kickball, broomball, tetherball, tug-of-war. The kids like to play steal-the-bacon."

"Steal-the-bacon."

"It's a tactical team game that rewards the skill and cunning of the individual."

"Team sport, is it?"

"Right."

"That's good. As I was saying, you've got your classroom and athletic space efficiently combined." I could hear, from somewhere on Jerry's end of the line, a sound like splashing water. I said, "That's very generous, Jerry, an airplane hangar," and he replied, "You'd be crazy to pass it up." Followed by another splash and Jerry saying, "Pete, I'm in the process of trying to unclog a sink over here. Water's been standing all day and I can't get any flow at all."

"Have you tried a snake?"

"No."

"You should try a snake." I gazed at my own sink's dark flecks of basin residue floating motionless on water that reached counter level. Was everybody in the neighborhood experiencing drainage difficulty? Were we all backed up? Was it a community thing?

The night outside was silent. No wind blew the leaves of trees against window glass or wall; no birds called. I could hear floorboards creaking overhead as Meredith made her way from bathroom to bed; and I heard the sound of Jerry's sink water, and of his breathing into the phone, as he asked me, "You wouldn't happen to have one of those snake things, would you, Pete?"

"Yes, I do. Would you like to borrow it?" But what was I saying? Jerry said, "That'd be great. What a lifesaver. I'll swing by and pick it up. Won't be a minute."

Now I'd done it. A man I couldn't trust was coming to get a household tool I was going to need myself.

Quickly I hid the plunger in the pantry, scraped the dinner dishes into the garbage, dumped the scraped-off dishes into the sink (thereby slopping oily water over the rim and onto my bare feet), squeezed in dish soap, swirled the water with my hand to make suds; and then, after concocting this absurd soaking-dish display aimed at hiding the truth of my own clogged drain from the soon-to-be-visiting Rotarian, with whom I would rather not risk a bonding experience, even of a mundane, plumbing-oriented variety (and to whom, also, I would rather not divulge the vulnerability evidenced by my own clogged drain, its revelation of material decay)—after staging this sink nonsense I went downstairs to the basement. There I paused a moment to admire my 1:32-scale, exhibition-quality balsa-and-Styrofoam cutaway reproduction of a Portuguese interrogation chamber (circa 1600), complete with rack, miniature shackles fashioned from spray-painted costume-jewelry chokers and clasps, and Q-tip puffs representing albino rats. Particularly effective were the sections of gray-painted "dungeon" wall fabricated from pieces of pressed Styrofoam swimming-pool kickboards burned with a soldering iron to give the impression of miniature mortise joints. I made a mental note to come down here and do some detail brushwork and free-form "chicken bone" accessorizing—the twin hallmarks of any successful scale model of this kind, I think—then forged deeper into the rank cellar, to the big metal closet where the tools lived. In the tool closet I discovered, to my surprise, not one but two plumber's snakes, coiled, lashed by lengths of identical nylon cording, and suspended from hooks. I left one and took its mate upstairs, and a moment later Jerry knocked and I opened the door and said, "Hello, I've got your snake. Want a cup of coffee?"

"Sure."

I put on water, got down cups, and gestured to Jerry, "Sit, please." Which Jerry did; he sat at the kitchen table and said, "Nice pit, Pete."

"Thanks." I suggested he get up close and check out Meredith's spear tips. Then I told him that, in spite of Meredith's excellent detail work, our pit was nothing compared to his; that his moat was very impressive from an overall engineering standpoint; that his design concept reinforced the thematic statement of the property in general, the house and grounds and so forth. I went on to note that the drawbridge had splendid workmanship in it, and that it was a rare thing to see that kind of wood-peg carpentry these days. I asked Jerry, "Tell me, do you anticipate problems with the moccasins? I mean, are they, do you think, likely to crawl out and, I don't know, whatever?"

Water steamed. How had I managed to allow, into my home, this man who released lethal vipers into a residential area? I could hear him exhaling through his mouth, when he insisted, "Precautions have been taken."

"Naturally. Of course. Milk and sugar?"

"Fine."

"Decaf okay?"

"Sure."

I measured grounds from bag to filter, took milk from the refrigerator, and said, "The funniest thing happened. I went down to the basement to get the plumber's snake, and there were two of them. How about that. Two snakes. I knew I had one, I remember buying it, in fact. But not two. It was strange. Two snakes."

"Let me get this straight. You thought you had one snake, but there were two?"

"Right."

"That *is* strange."

The pot whistled. I poured boiling water and considered the Freedom Field issue. Specifically, the wisdom of broaching this difficult topic in my own kitchen. You could hear everything in this old house, and Meredith might or might not have been soundly sleeping, and Jerry's airplane hangar proposal, quixotic though it was, might appeal to my wife. Why risk that? No, my "home school" concept was definitely the way to go. Better keep mum on the subject of Freedom Field. Coffee dripped and I said, witlessly, "At any rate, now if I get a clog while you've got one snake, I'll still be fine, because I'll have the other."

"That's the truth."

"That'd be quite a coincidence, wouldn't it?"

"I'm of a mind, Pete, that there is no such thing as coincidence. I agree with some of the fellows down at Rotary who say the cosmos abounds in mysteries invisible to us in our waking state, worlds within worlds, and that our task in life is to open our inner eyes, perceive reality in its totality, and embrace the million levels of Universal Consciousness."

It was my first indication of the nonsecular nature of the local chapter of Rotary International. It worried me. I sipped coffee and listened to Jerry say, "Friday we're sponsoring a theriomorphism workshop luncheon at the Holiday Inn—why don't you and your wife come as my guests?"

"Oh, gee, well."

"This is going to be the Rotary luncheon of the year, not counting your informative and entertaining talk on persuasive methods of the medieval Inquisition. You don't want to miss this. And Pete?"

"Yeah?"

"It's potluck, so, if you could, if you wouldn't mind contributing a salad?"

"A salad." Why didn't I just say no? Jerry offered, "Or dessert. Dessert or a salad, whichever's easier. Would that be possible?"

"Sure, a salad."

A nice tossed green one with fresh cherry tomatoes, lots of cukes, red and green bell pepper, basil, watercress, fennel, and many leaves of other things. Together Meredith and I and a crowd of red-faced Rotarians and their well-dressed wives (Rotary Anns) sat around hotel banquet tables and listened to a visiting anthropology professor at the junior college say, "Pick an animal, any animal, fish, fowl, beast. Concentrate on aspects of the animal. Is it big? Small? Cute? Does it eat other animals? What color fur? If the animal is a bird, what color are its feathers? What song does it sing?"

"This is stupid," I whispered to Meredith.

"It's your fault we're here. Why don't you give it a chance?"

The anthropologist said, "Why don't we all think about it for a minute? Okay, everybody got one?"

"Yes," "No," "Wait," people said. Meredith whispered, "What's yours?"

"I don't know, what's yours?"

"Coelacanth."

"The prehistoric fish?"

"I need a volunteer," declared the professor. Meredith raised her hand, and the man at the podium said, "Yes, back there. Tell us your name and the name of the animal you've chosen to become today."

"Meredith Robinson. Coelacanth. It's a kind of fish that scientists believed extinct until one was caught off the coast of Africa."

"Excellent. Come forward. Sit here. Would someone please dim the lights?" I watched Rotary guys watch my wife. Bill Nixon, Tom Thompson, Abraham de Leon, Dick Morton, Terry Heinemann, Robert Isaac—all the usuals, plus others. Jerry and his wife, Rita, sat up front. The professor soothingly said, "Close your eyes, breathe deeply, and tell us about the coelacanth. Everybody else, let's all breathe deeply too, and be thinking about our own animals. Go ahead, Meredith."

"Well, it's five feet long, deep slate blue, with bony, protruding fins and big jaws with scary teeth. It goes back seventy million years. It moves slowly, it dwells in dark water." The professor nodded. Audience members inched forward in their seats. Meredith said, "At night it swims upside down with its head pointed to the sea bottom, bobbing along."

"A feeding technique?"

"Maybe."

"How's the water?" I could see Meredith's head settle forward as she softly answered, "Cold."

"Feel the cold. Breathe that cold. Inhale that water. What do you feel?"

"Colors."

"Colors?"

"Blue, black, indigo."

The anthropologist stepped from the stage and came forward into the crowd gathered around tables set with plates that were littered with discarded skeletons of poached red snapper (the luncheon's fish course, provided by Jerry and Rita); he collected white small bones from several plates and carried the bones back to the stage area and scattered them in a circle around my wife's chair. He produced a portable cassette deck and loaded a tape that played hollow drum rhythms. He intoned along with the drums, "There is a circle of sea and you are in it, Coelacanth, bobbing above the ocean floor where the lonely crab rests on rocks where no mollusk grows. Blue squid drift on black tides lit by lanternfish. The solitary shark pays a visit but that doesn't concern you. You are the last of the ancients. Swim your swim!"

I watched Meredith's head and shoulders gently moving. Rita Henderson clutched her husband's arm. Men I knew and others I didn't sat still with their wives, all focused on my wife's feet suddenly dancing like bottom fish above bone-strewn hotel carpet. The visiting professor commanded, "Rise, Coelacanth. Cavort in the blue cold."

Meredith did rise. She hopped from foot to foot inside her private bone circle, head hanging, arms shivering, hands with tapering fingers churning air—she was working up a sweat.

People in the audience swayed along with the echoing taped drumbeats. Everywhere, heads oscillated and feet tapped. Abraham de Leon was particularly into it: his mouth fell open, his tongue wagged, his body visibly trembled. I couldn't imagine what kind of animal he was. And Tom Thompson! Unlike Abe, Tom did not tremble so much as quake. He bounced in his chair in a violent manner that caused other guests to stare at him and cough suggestively, but Tom was immersed in his own head and taking no notice; and soon the whole room was shaking to the sounds of drums getting louder and the instructor's voice calling out, "Single-celled protozoa, insects, small birds and wildfowl; warm-blooded animals and sleepy reptiles; crustacea, fish, aquatic mammalia—everybody join in with Meredith the coelacanth, let's go, creatures, dance it!" Rotarians and their wives staggered from chairs and wobbled to the front of the room and encircled my wife in a bestial conga in which I alone did not participate. I remained at my table. I hadn't even chosen an animal.

The visiting professor came over and said, "Excuse me, is she with you?"

"Yes."

"In some societies, special individuals are selected to enter alternate states of consciousness and ritually explore the spirit realm. Most of the people in that conga line merely imagine themselves as animals, but she's actually *become* her animal. I've seen it before. It's rare. She's a natural. She has a gift."

"Really?"

"I'd like to spend time with her, monitor her rhythms, observe entry conditions, coach her in the methodology of closure. The novice can easily become lost between worlds and, in rare cases, suffer psychotic episodes. Trance experience is something our culture doesn't prepare us for."

From the conga line: grunts and hoots rising above the rumbling of many feet. Meredith in the vortex danced. The professor said, "She's learning to swim."

"I was learning to swim," Meredith said later. Sweaty businessmen and their wives gathered around. All eyes were on my wife, who told the crowd, "Water held me. I was able to accept myself as a fish, and to feel the pain of living. I didn't need assurances that I was worthy of love."

And at home that night, she told me, "As a person, I always needed someone to hold me, but as a fish I was buoyant, able to hold myself. Now I'm a little buoyant, but I also need to be held, because I feel heavy inside. I miss the friends I made in the ocean."

We were lying in bed with the covers pulled up. We held cups of hot milk with honey.

"Friends?"

"Other coelacanths. More than friends, actually. One was my mother and one was my father, and I had schools of brothers and sisters. I knew them, and they knew me. They didn't wonder where I'd come from, because I'd always been there with them. As I am now. Even while lying with you, here, in our house, in our bed, I'm down there in cold water, swimming upside down, brushing against another coelacanth, making my presence felt and feeling the presence of another, before going off to a deep place to look for something precious."

"Something precious?"

"A rock or a piece of coral. Something smooth, something shiny, something black."

Her breaths grew slow and deep, her breasts rose and fell. Katydids made scratchy noises in the pollenating mango outside our window. Wind blew a tree branch scraping claw-like against the house. A small time passed. I gave my sleeping wife a peck on the cheek, then threw off the covers, got up and dressed, and padded downstairs to the night-light-lit kitchen, where I sipped instant decaf and peered into the freezer at vaporescent packages of food piled in a heap atop the collected remains of Jim Kunkel.

I dug my hand beneath Tupperware containers and alligator baggies. I touched a cold baseball that must've been the heart, and a small item that was probably a gland, and next to that a larger thing. The liver? I grabbed the extra-big package and heaved it out. It wasn't Jim's liver, it was his foot—a substantial piece of flesh, 12 DD or E at least. It felt good to hold. It weighed a lot. I tossed it in the air and it flipped neatly end over end and fell back into my hand. Nice. The foot, not being an organ, did not seem *momentous* in the way Jim's frozen heart, liver, adrenal glands, lung tissue, and genitals seemed momentous. To be sure, the Foot has its place in myth and legend; it carries psychohistoric weight. In our culture, the Foot as Symbol is not unimportant. Nevertheless, for me, at that point in time (hours, only, since Meredith's initiatory ichthyomorphic trance experience with its insomnia-inducing implications concerning self-identity and marital compatibility—"It's like sex, Pete. Once you've entered that other body, you're always there, even when you're not. I'm not a coelacanth, I'm a person and I'm here, this is where I am, this is who I am. I'm Meredith. But I'm a coelacanth, too."

"Can I become one, can I come with you?"

"That's the thing, Pete, you have to be there already, and you weren't. I'm sorry, honey.")—at that point in time, as I was saying, Jim's frozen foot seemed perfect for an inaugural burial excursion. I could figure out how to do things right, and not rush. I could work out the funerary process, the digging and lowering into the earth and chanting of sacred texts, in a more relaxed way with a foot than with probably, say, a heart. Yes. With the foot I had an opportunity to get comfortable with the ritual aspect of nighttime burial. Later I could progress to Jim's frozen hand and the more difficult (symbolically speaking) internal parts. The viscera.

I figured I'd just chuck the slightly freezer-burned foot in a knapsack and walk around town until I came to a place that felt right for burial.

I left the house at around midnight and crept up the driveway to the road. I wore canvas sneakers, athletic socks, safari shorts, a tee-shirt, and the bright purple knapsack containing Jim's cold, hard foot, a garden trowel, a box of candles and matches to light them, a library copy of *The Egyptian Book of the Dead,* and some fig bars for a snack. The darkness that night was total; clouds obscured the stars and moon; the only light descended from streetlamps spilling pools of white over damp leaves of roadside shrubs, shiny parked cars, and the road itself, where I walked alone over gravel that crunched underfoot.

At Wisteria I turned left toward town. I passed a vacant lot, which I rejected because of a chain-link fence I'd have to scale, and because several lamplit windows in surrounding houses gave easy viewer access to that neglected, overgrown locale. After a while I came to the Chamber of Commerce.

Here I turned right onto Water Street, which is where Meredith's mother lives. No lights on at Helen's bungalow. I hurried past Meredith's mother's Oldsmobile, and continued on to where Water dead-ends into Osprey. Right on Osprey would lead me to Jerry Henderson's. I went left. A sea breeze was blowing up the road. Osprey Avenue runs all the way to the ocean, about a mile, but I didn't want to go to the ocean; I desired dark soil for this virgin implantation, not grainy wet sand overrun with fiddler crabs. So at the next intersection I veered right off Osprey and walked along Pompano Place. Here were more and more elaborate pits; every householder along this moderately wealthy drive had installed one. And there were walls bordering Pompano too: cinder block, coral rock, and timbers solidly rising, garnished with barbed wire and alarm-system warning decals.

At the end of the street sat the home of a former pupil, a boy named Ben Webster who, years before, had distinguished himself with a science fair essay on Annual Coastal Erosion Due to Global Temperature Shifts and Resultant Polar Ice Cap Meltdown Contributing to Rising Sea Levels.

No light shone from the Websters' palm-shrouded house girded in electric fencing. I passed by and entered the gumbo-limbo hammock known as Turtle Pond Park.

But let me briefly pause. Let me take a moment before starting on what happened that night with the foot, the candles, and the book, to reflect on the many things that had brought me to this point, this nocturnal action. As, in fact, I did that very night, standing at the dark entrance to the impenetrable-seeming public glade—I paused a moment, there at the stone gate marking the park's western perimeter, to let my eyes adjust to the primordial dark beneath the hammock canopy; but also to consider the meanings of things, and to experience, if I could, wrapped in gloom, a few realizations about the consciousness of personality. It was something I'd been thinking about ever since the night of the ex-mayor's death. Now, standing outside Turtle Pond Park, getting ready to go in and carry out the promise hastily made to the doomed man, I discovered inside my heart a radiant sensation of connectedness: to Jim Kunkel, and to his, and my, and all our ancestors going back to the first voyagers in the realm of the psyche: the pre-Christian fertility cults of the Nile, of the Danube Basin, of Asia and Africa. It was subtle at first, a tingling kind of mild appreciation of my relationship to others, of ambitions and acts determining not only my own destiny but the destinies of people requiring care and compassion from me: Meredith, the kids of the third grade, the townspeople who might one day cast their ballots in support of Pete Robinson for mayor. The foot—which was thawing, incidentally, at a rapid rate, leaking onto my fig bars, though I didn't know this until later—the foot seemed suddenly symbolically freighted with all our aspirations and dreams, the collective dreams of a community. Indeed, it was as if it were not Jim Kunkel's foot being buried, not Jim's foot at all, but a flesh-and-blood vessel containing the Hopes of Men—Jim, me, anybody and everybody—for a better, wiser world that might spring from soil made fertile by blood and bone. Such were my thoughts. Imagine my chagrin when, immediately upon stepping past the stone threshold to the dark and misty park, I heard the husky voice of my former star pupil, Ben Webster himself, calling out to me in a stage whisper, "Hey,

Mr. Robinson, is that you? What are you doing here? Get away from there. You're going to step on a mine."

"Hello?"

"Over here," from behind the bushes.

I stepped lightly. "Ben, it's late. What are you doing up at this time of night?"

"Give me a break, Mr. Robinson. I'm not a kid anymore." He wore jungle fatigues and combat boots and a dark beret; his face was smeared with charcoal. He wore a holster. He said, "Stay low, be quiet, follow me," then proceeded to duck-walk into deeper recesses of forest. I hunkered down. Clearly Ben was intimate with this marshy topography trimmed in elephant-ear ferns and hanging mosses; he led an easy path beneath silhouetted black limbs hanging low; his steps generated no sound. Mine, of course, reverberated. I said, "Sorry, I'm not very good at this kind of thing," and Ben whispered back, "Concentrate on step placement, Mr. Robinson. You'll get the hang of it. There's a big root up here, watch out."

"Ben, did you say mines?"

"Claymores. That jerk Mr. Benson planted them. We've located some but we don't have the technology to disarm or remove them."

"We?"

"Me and my dad."

"How is your dad?" I knew Chuck Webster from PTA meetings. Years before, when Ben was little and attending grade school, Chuck Webster had been a friendly and supportive presence at our bimonthly open-house conferences concerning core curriculum and dress codes. His input was always appreciated by the teaching staff, who felt from him a sensitivity unusual in the lay community, to the diverse and often contradictory objectives—the whole "socialization versus individuation: which to encourage?" problem, with its attendant classroom dilemmas around issues of fair grading for "fast" and "slow" learners, how to reward effort, whether to encourage interdisciplinarianism, etc.—of primary education. Ben said, "Dad's okay, I guess. Why don't you ask him yourself?"

"Friend or foe?" a man's voice called from the shadows.

"It's me, Dad," Ben whispered back.

Chuck Webster stepped out. He wore a drab and dark military night-ordnance ensemble exactly like his son's. Additionally, the elder Webster carried a semiautomatic assault weapon slung over his shoulder. He looked intimidating behind his rakish, thin mustache, but he sounded hospitable, neighborly, when he said, "Well, if it isn't Pete Robinson. What brings you to the park, Pete?"

"Oh, nothing." Right away I was aware that this was a stupid thing to declare, even to apparently nonhostile types, within an arena, as this clearly was, of suspicion. I said, "So, what's up?"

"You're lucky you didn't lose a leg or your foot, Pete. You're lucky Ben was nearby."

We were standing in a clearing. An owl hooted. The night felt unseasonably warm.

"Pete, we've got surplus protective gear back at the house, I'm sure we could fit you up. It would be a shame for anything to happen to you. You're a valuable asset to this community. You have to teach our youngsters to make a better world than the one we've made. Am I right?"

"Right, Chuck."

"Actually, Dad, Mr. Robinson always spent a lot of class time lecturing about war and killing and torture and things," Ben Webster said.

"I'm sure your teacher was merely highlighting the tragic and beautiful history of human conflict. Isn't that the case, Pete?"

"Something like that."

Chuck pointed through the trees. "There's plenty of struggle tonight in Turtle Pond Park, Pete."

Sure enough, I could detect distant shadowy forms of people moving. I felt remorse—it was momentary, a swift and transitory psychic experience containing awareness of various realities: the reality of the foot; of my growing guilt and shame around the issue of my failure, the night of Jim's death, to intervene and turn the tide of vengeance, to administer beneficent justice; the sad fact of Meredith's coelacanth dreams, her drum-accompanied departure for mental seas where our life together was beside the point. And the school situation. Ben's presence brought up all the feelings of contrition I'd been repressing, concerning my clear willingness to sit around in my comfortable kitchen and formulate "home school" plans, then do nothing in the way of follow-up. Chuck Webster was right, I had a job to do. And if I got it together now, the home school that is—if I got it together now, we could be looking at practically a complete school year ahead.

I knelt beside Ben, who was observing, through infrared goggles, a mini-battalion of allegedly invidious neighbors snaking along a narrow footpath that traversed the southern sector of the park.

"Hey Ben, how'd you like to be a big player in the future of this town?"

"Me?"

"Your science fair essay on rising sea levels lives in my memory as one of the finest examples of third-grade student research I've encountered in my career. You're a dedicated thinker who understands intellectual thoroughness and the value of knowledge. I'd be proud to have your help recruiting students for the school I plan to open."

"School?"

"Admittedly your credentials are thin. You're not a high school graduate yet. What grade would you be now, anyway?"

"Tenth."

"That's pretty far along. Plus you have real-world experience. That's worth a lot. Let's say you have graduate equivalency."

"Okay."

"Now you're eligible for employment within the educational system."

"Great."

"I'll need your Social Security number. I'll have to see a birth certificate. We'll start you out at a reasonable hourly rate to be negotiated later."

We shook hands, and Ben whispered across the clearing, "Dad, guess what, I got a job!" But his father was nowhere to be seen.

Ben scampered across the clearing. He scanned the perimeter with the night-vision goggles. He called out in earnest, hushed tones, "Dad, Dad."

Nighttime shadows dappled the forest's undergrowth and

ground; the whole world challenged perception. I could distinguish, with certainty, only Ben, some nearby branches, and the nickel shimmer on the barrel of the unholstered handgun in his hand, when Ben came close and whispered, "Thanks for the career opportunity, Mr. Robinson, but Dad and I made a vow. If he's harmed, I must hunt down and discharge a bullet into the heart of the person responsible."

The dark shapes previously roving the southern trail were no longer in evidence. I tried to make light of the situation. "Look, your father probably just went off to conduct some reconnaissance."

Fear was in the boy's voice when he said, "Dad wouldn't go on maneuvers without telling me."

He stepped into the woods. "Can't hang around. Dad's in trouble. Check you later."

"Hey, wait a minute, Ben. What's going on with you guys and the Bensons?"

But it was too late, he was gone, vanished into the shrubs, leaving me alone and without insight into the apparent disharmony between the two families.

I stood beneath the spooky trees. The night was quiet. I took off the knapsack, reached in and fished out the trowel. Clouds parted overhead to reveal a few stars. The clearing was, actually, an ideal burial setting—it had all the right qualities. Could I reasonably risk shoveling earth, lighting candles, and reciting incantations in a vicinity likely to be overrun by kin groups brandishing private arsenals? Yes. There was something fitting about it. It was my purpose: to render a symbolic narrative of regeneration, using pieces of Jim as literal embodiments of life transformed—in this case the Foot, which walks over land, alerting us to textures, temperatures, feelings. The burial of Jim's foot would underscore the pain of physical existence, while attesting to the mortality of the middle-to-high-income households currently vying for control of Turtle Pond Park.

Down I knelt. Twigs and leaves and rocks were everywhere. I heaped them into a pile. The cleared tract was level and hard against the rounded blade of the trowel plunging in, scraping noisily; I crouched low and bent over, using my body as a baffle against the grainy rasp of steel on dirt. Cautiously I dug. Pebbles bit into my knees. It wasn't long before I had a sore back and neck. There was a lot of tension that night in the park, all the tension that naturally accompanies proximity to armed strife. Sweat ran into my eyes, and I leaned back and raised a hand to wipe away the salt sting; and I reflected on Chuck Webster's eerie disappearance. He'd been standing no more than twenty feet from where Ben and I had convened to talk business. Suddenly, he was gone. It wasn't the sort of thing you wanted to have happening in a civic recreational space.

I set aside the trowel and rummaged in the pack, took out *The Egyptian Book of the Dead* and placed it beside the burial site. The plastic-wrapped foot was soggy. Holding it up, now, up above the shallow hole in the ground (fingers caressing instep, thumb pressing ankle), I experienced, for the second time that night, a thrill of attachment to the man it had belonged to, and I knew I was doing the right thing, bringing Jim's foot to the embattled park. This little clearing, like Jim's own neatly clipped lawn that dark night of his passing, was sacred space.

I laid the foot beside the grave. Salty ocean breezes bent limbs of trees into arabesques, making the world a church. I lit a candle, opened the book at random, and read aloud:

"'I am a shining being, and a dweller in light, who hath been created and hath come into existence from the limbs of the god.'"

Not bad. But what did it mean, really? There was no way for me to know, only to speculate. I'm not an Egyptologist. My previous studies of comparative religion have been confined to medieval Christian variants prominent in the Germanic and Mediterranean regions during assorted state-sanctioned periods of witch and heretic hunting, when ecclesiastical nuance determined the destiny of illiterate, cowed populations. The Inquisition is an archetypal instance of nonsecular terrorism—it's a template for institutionalized cruelties that have abided throughout modern history. Back when Jim was still alive, back before the ex-mayor, without warning or explanation, launched those shoulder-fired Stinger missiles—and where did a guy like Kunkel get that kind of firepower, anyway? Clearly, high office has its perks—into the Botanical Garden reflecting pool, thus bringing down all manner of pain—a week or so before this happened I gave my standard talk, at a Rotary luncheon, on this very topic: "The Barbarity of the Past: How Ancient Fears Inform the Organizing Principles and Moral Values of Modern Life."

That lecture, I realized now, holding the sputtering birthday candle in one hand and the archaic burial manual in the other—that lecture was a kind of starting point in the chain of circumstance that had brought me to this dangerous glade to perform esoteric nocturnal rites.

Could I ever have seen any of this coming, that late-summer Friday at the Holiday Inn?

It was a capacity crowd. Jerry and Rita Henderson sat up front. Bill and Barbara Nixon lounged at a neighboring table. I noticed Abraham de Leon picking crumbs from his beard. Tom Thompson chugged cups of coffee. And there was Jim Kunkel himself, looking patriarchal and well tanned but also a bit feeble in yellow pants and golf shirt and shiny white shoes. At that time the old ex-mayor had only a few days to live, but who could know this? Everybody seemed slightly stunned from the volumes of delicately poached blowfish they'd tucked away. It was a tough house. I sipped from my water glass, cleared my throat, leaned close to the microphone and said, "So you see, these dread ministers, the Inquisitors, inflicted every extreme of ruthlessness on reputed heretics, many mere petty criminals or political agitators, not religious activists at all. Ruthlessness on behalf of orthodoxy. It's the old story. What's interesting in the case of the Inquisition, and it is a phenomenon that has been demonstrated time and again, in diverse theaters, even right up into the modern era, is the ready accessibility of holy text as a tool of repression."

Meredith at the back of the big banquet room smiled encouragement. I went to the portable blackboard behind the podium, picked up a piece of chalk, and began sketching diagrams. "Okay, the rack, an unpretentious stretching device, mechanically rudimentary, employed in the regular daily work of coercion and castigation. The rack's primary social impact was arguably psychological as well as physical. As long as the authorities had recourse to such an instrument, with liberty to use it at their discretion, which is to say at the slightest provocation, the lay community, understandably, inhabited a condition of low-grade panic." I raised the chalk to fill in picturesque details: "crank," "berth," "leather thongs," and so on. People shifted in their chairs, leaned forward to get a better view. Jerry Henderson was engrossed, peering at the board. Bill Nixon perked right up. It's difficult to overestimate the value, as a teaching aid, of pictures. When I used to give this almost identical though considerably more elementary "Inquisition talk" to my third-graders—always a hard-to-please bunch—they, like these grown-ups assembled at the Holiday Inn for Friday luncheon, became enthralled, absolutely, as though on cue, when I marched to the board and picked up the chalk and made fine white renderings of dungeon environments. Suddenly the old classroom would fall silent. No gum popping, no spitballs sailing, no notes being passed. The kids' eager questions reflected a deep concern for history's artifacts.

"Did the torturers leave the people on that thing for a long time?"

"Did you get taller?"

"Could you get torn in half?"

I could sense my adult audience's yearning to raise their own inquiries, as I casually dropped the chalk in the chalk tray and returned to the podium. I watched Rita Henderson brush lint from her purple blouse. Jerry folded and refolded a napkin. Jim Kunkel chewed a toothpick. I let all these people contemplate the past. "In those days you were guilty until proven innocent." I took another sip of water. Heads wagged, a fork scraped a plate, ice rattled.

"Questions, anyone?"

Jim raised his hand. "Pete, would you say that the past lives on in the present?"

"Certainly, brutality has long been the order of the day, Jim."

"Yep," he said. Then Barbara Nixon—not a bad-looking woman, incidentally—spoke up. "Mr. Robinson, are you saying that ours is a cruel culture?"

"Something like that."

"I can't accept that. We're good people here. We care about one another."

"Oh, give it a rest," Jim growled at her.

Everyone regarded the ex-mayor.

"Excuse me?" from Bill.

"There's no love here," was all Jim said.

Bill told him, "I think you owe my wife an apology."

Barbara nudged her husband, "Forget it honey, he's just a crazy old man."

To which Jim replied, to both or either of the Nixons, or maybe—who knows?—to the room in general, "Fuck off."

At which point Jerry broke in and diplomatically asked, "What I want to know, Pete, is could you be torn in half on one of those racks?"

"Probably not. There were, however, methods of accomplishing such punishment."

"Drawing and quartering," said the ex-mayor. There was a feeling, in the room, of unease. I pressed on: "Precisely. The accused is harnessed by hand and foot to four hardy beasts of burden, which are then encouraged by drovers to walk or trot away in different directions."

"That's a powerful image," said Rita Henderson. Abraham

de Leon, who rumor had it was conducting an on-again, off-again affair with his friend Jerry's wife, added, with an air of nonchalance, "Yes."

Everyone nodded agreement. I elaborated: "It's an image that speaks not only to physical but emotional fragmentation. We say, 'I'm torn,' to describe confusion over complex choices. Once upon a time, individuals who challenged received truths were literally torn by oxen or horses. Modern man's psyche is figuratively torn by internal dilemmas posed in the struggle to escape unconscious prohibitions and taboos passed down from generation to generation."

"Sexual taboos?" Barbara Nixon suggested. Did I see her wink? I looked back at Meredith, who was grinning. Bill Nixon was grinning too. Or sneering. Barbara didn't seem to notice her husband's sideways gaze on her; she smiled widely and asked, "Is that what you mean, Mr. Robinson?"

Before I could reply, Bill broke in, rudely, "Of course that's what he means."

"I didn't ask you, honey."

It was an embarrassing moment. Why can't couples behave? I said, "Sure, sexual, spiritual, intellectual, whatever."

"The point being that we're not supposed to explore our true feelings, or discover our innermost selves." This from Jim, who rose from his chair and gestured dramatically with a water glass held high; cold water sloshed over the undulating glass's rim, splashing the carpet and threatening nearby diners, who ducked away. Jerry Henderson cautioned, "Easy with that water, Mr. Mayor," as icy liquid splashed in a crystal arc over Tom Thompson's crew-cut head.

"Hey, watch it," Tom said.

Jim replaced the glass on the table and grunted, "Sorry." Tom dried himself with a napkin. Rita Henderson clutched her husband's hand—tightly. And Barbara Nixon looked up at me looking back at Meredith. We all listened to the decrepit voice of the ex-mayor, flatly proclaiming, "We're all murderers here."

At that moment the banquet hall's wide metal doors swung open and Bob and Betsy Isaac entered from the kitchen, bearing silver trays laden with pie topped with generous helpings of whipped cream. "Ah, ooh," people said. In this way, beneath sounds of eating, Jim's solemn commentary was buried. For the moment at least. Many times after that day I pondered Kunkel's words. Holding the thawing foot above the grave, I felt engaged in an enactment of prophesy, and I knew my midnight burial signified not only community rebirth and regeneration but also personal genesis. Entombing Jim's foot was an essential step toward assuming the mantle of civic leadership, becoming mayor. Campaign poster slogans filled my mind: PETE ROBINSON FOR PEACE ON EARTH. PETE ROBINSON, A STEP TOWARD PARADISE.

The foot grave was two feet deep, not traditional depth, but deep enough (probably?) to discourage animals. I lowered the foot into darkness. I left it tightly freezer-wrapped—the twist-tied plastic, washed in leaking fluids, served admirably as a makeshift shroud. And I set aside *The Egyptian Book of the Dead*. It was wrong to use it. Wasn't I just appropriating text from one culture, blindly applying it within another, merely to suit a private agenda? Better to honor my burial scenario with a song born of the moment.

I improvised: "Proud foot, never again will you walk over

grass or road or sidewalk. Once you carried a man on his daily rounds, you carried him through life. Now his work is done. Carry us, the living, carry us forward into knowledge of the heart's truth."

And I scooped dirt, held my hands over the grave, let the black earth trickle down onto the foot. I felt, then, a creepy intimation of surveillance. As if, from the shadows behind the trees, someone watched. How might this ceremony appear to a stranger? Certainly people bury things. Deceased pets, for instance. I packed loose soil and called out, "Hello?" But there was only stillness and a smell of ozone sweetly lofting in on a wind; and, from the west, the sound of thunder, its heavy echo rolling in from over the wetlands bordering town. Clouds eclipsed the moon and stars. I stuck a twig into the burial mound. It wasn't much, only an obscure marker. Nevertheless I bent my head prayerfully over it and intoned these words: "Herein lies Jim Kunkel's left foot, symbolizing leadership, fearlessness, creativity, and strength. Soon it will become dust. But the spirit of Jim shall rise up and walk into our homes and our hearts, it will guide us out of darkness."

Rain struck the canopy of leaves. I groped for library book, trowel, candles, the purple knapsack. I eased aside thorny stems, stepped tentatively onto fallen leaves that sponged underfoot. Immediately the soles of my Keds sank deep into sucking mud. Mud that was, apparently, mined. There was no way of knowing where to walk. Quietly I whispered, "Okay, buried foot, I've done my part, now you do yours and get me out of here."

Sure enough, a voice spoke. "Pete."

I looked up to see a man with tangled hair. He was standing

beside a tree. His clothes were soiled, dirt messed his face and arms. He was immense. He said, "It's me, Pete, Ray. Ray Conover."

"Ray?"

The man stepped forward, leaned in close. "You wouldn't recognize me, would you, Pete?"

"Uh, no."

He raised his arms and waved his hands, wildly, for emphasis. "Grief changes a person, Pete. Once I was happy. I was. Look at me. I've aged, my teeth hurt. You, your world is intact. Oh, you're out here tonight doing unfathomable things. But tomorrow you'll be in a warm bed beside a person you love. I don't have that anymore. This is my home now."

"The park? You live in the park? There's a war going on here."

"Yeah, well." How sad the man sounded. How dejected. I decided to be up front with him. In a firm but cordial voice, I said, "Listen, Ray, I'd love to spend some time talking, but I also want to get out of these woods."

"Sure, Pete. No problem."

And so off we went, rain smacking our heads and the slushy ground underfoot. From the tops of trees, narrow vines descended; Ray and I made our way through their tangle, clutching twisted tree limbs for balance, stepping around roots. It was slippery going through those woods. Everywhere life crowded in. I placed my feet where Ray'd set his, and with each step tensed for a buried trigger's click. It was awful. Ray said, "I watched what you were doing, Pete. The burial. The eulogy. Why, Pete?"

"I want a better world."

"So you buried a foot."

"Not just a foot. More. Much more."

I tripped on a root. This was terrifying under the circumstances. A few minutes later lightning struck nearby, lighting the woods instantaneously neon—I was certain it was the end, and hit the dirt and rolled, coming to rest sprawled piteously on my stomach in a patch of weeds, my hands covering the back of my head, the way they're supposed to, reflexively, when a bomb goes off. Ray came over, stood above me, said, "Whoopsie!" and helped me to my feet. Pine needles and leafy rot adhered to my clothes and skin; I was covered in mud. I brushed off as best I could, but it was more like smearing body paint. I asked, "So, Ray, what can you tell me about this Benson-Webster thing?"

"Not much. It's the old story. Someone does something and someone else does something back. After that things have a life of their own. Who can say what it's about anymore? The Bensons have the southern triangle from Lighthouse Point to the boathouse. The bandshell, goldfish pond, and Japanese pagoda belong to the Websters. This is neutral territory we're in right now. Watch out, there's a log ahead."

"Thanks." I stepped over and we moved on. Ray told me, "Other parkside families are taking sides. The Lloyds with the Websters, the Glazers with the Bensons. Coalitions are developing."

"They've captured Chuck Webster."

"That's too bad, Chuck's a good guy. There's a sinkhole up here, careful. Remember that time Paul and Cindy Garrison's daughter Mindy fell off Jack Conley's glass-bottom reef-tour boat, and no one realized it until everybody saw Mindy through the glass, about to get run over by the propeller, and Chuck dove in and fetched her out and gave her mouth-to-mouth? I always admired that."

Ray ducked beneath a branch. I ducked after him. He guided a path through brambles and ferns that gave onto a wall of leaves hanging like black curtains. "Here we are, my friend," he said, stepping out of the forest and onto a narrow white beach: the peninsular tip of Turtle Pond Park. We'd gone away from, not toward, town. Waves were coming in close. Salt smells blended with the complex atmospheric odors that accompany rough weather in this part of the world, forming a cool perfume evocative of the miseries of childhood. Here in the wide open the wind was fierce, and it didn't take long to get soaked. Ray hollered, "My world's gone, Pete. There's no logic left. Kunkel was crazy, he caused deaths. Miriam's. Other people's."

"Ray, I know you're in pain. I wish it hadn't happened, hadn't had to happen. Jim was warning us. He was sending a message."

Ray shivered, his teeth chattered. "There is no way that I can accept that."

I reached into the knapsack and brought out *The Egyptian Book of the Dead*. "Got a light?" I scooped a hollow in the sand, then tore pages from the book and crumpled them into a pile in the shallow campfire depression. I knelt over, guarding paper from pelting rain, and said, "Hate to do this to a book, especially a library copy." Ray said, "Well, anyway, no one except you is ever going to want to check that out." He crouched down and butane-lit a page; as the fire caught and kindled I added more pages; I kept ripping out text. Surf broke and rolled nearly to our shoes. We warmed our hands above incendiary hieroglyphics soaring aloft on convective heat, tumbling wetly up the beach, and Ray told me, "I want a better world too, Pete."

"Then help me. Join my school. Become a teacher."

"Me?"

"You have so much to offer. You can stock an aquarium. Take the kids wading in tidal pools, go snorkling over the reef. The pay's not great but the rewards are priceless." I had a feeling, as I said this, of conviction: the home school was more than a kitchen table fancy. By pitching the vision to potential colleagues—first Ben, now Ray—I made intention tangible; and I knew, whether the feral biologist signed on or not—I knew the school would come to pass.

Ray felt my enthusiasm. "I could teach?"

"Why not?"

"I'm a researcher."

"You know things, Ray. Look around. The ocean, the sky, this terrible weather. It's all happening. The world at work. Your world."

"Beautiful, isn't it?"

I ripped more pages. Lightning struck over the water. I counted slowly to seven before hearing thunder rumble in above waves crashing onto nearby rocks littered with cast-up debris. That meant the storm was seven miles out to sea. So it was moving away. As if that mattered. Everything was drenched. The fire was a lost cause. I raised my hands with palms turned upward and cupped to catch rain, and drank a libation of sweet rainwater. Ray, too, cupped his hands and drank. He exclaimed, "In the beginning of time, this is what there was."

"Ray, are you hungry? Break bread with me."

That's when I discovered my fig bars' contaminated condition. Not by eating one myself but by watching Ray eat one. He spat fig. Talk about your difficult moments. But wasn't it fitting?—the bereaved taking into his mouth the blood of his wife's executioner. Ray couldn't see the elegance of this symmetry, he was too busy going berserk from the putridity of blood and rot that had entered his mouth via a leaked-on fig bar; and he was saying words to me, attempting to anyway—something garbled I couldn't quite make out but that was, judging from tone and inflection, harshly accusatory. He got up then and started walking away. Staggering, actually, was more like what he was doing; he staggered, retching, down the beach. What could I say? Let him go. I have to admit I was relieved to find myself alone again. But I felt sorry, too, that our evening had come to this distressing close, because, crummy weather aside—wasn't the weather an integral part of the evening? Hadn't the weather in some ways *defined* the evening?—rotten weather aside, our hour together on the beach, watching the world and feeling exposed to elemental forces, had been, as Ray himself had claimed, beautiful.

At dawn the storm passed. It was half a mile to Midnight Pass and the old humpbacked bridge sportsmen favor for grouper and snook. Walking on sand was tiring; I rested on a bridge railing and let the heat of morning dry me. No one out fishing today, which was odd, seeing as it was a Saturday. Perhaps it was the wrong time of day. Maybe wisdom or fear regarding storms kept the cane-pole fishermen home in their beds. I'm not much of an angler myself. I trekked along the South Main flood canal, checking the black water for nictitating opalescent eyelids of partly submerged gators. South Main intersects with palm-lined Osprey Avenue. Left on Osprey, it was a mile to town. My shoes were full of sand; I took them off and banged them against a tree. After the Tarpon Bank Savings and Loan I crossed an unfortified yard—a few still remained—coming out between two birdbaths onto Water Street. Three blocks away sat the Southshore branch of the public library, opposite which I paused to enter the tall bushes and, checking to make sure no one could see, urinated quickly, before zipping up and coming out to study the library bulletin board advertising poetry clubs, garden societies, yard sales, bake sales (including one to raise money for the failing library system), babysitting services, papier-mâché workshops, housepainting, handgun seminars, car repair, and lawn work. A printed handbill announced that night's big town meeting out at Terry Heinemann's Clam Castle. Another poster, elegantly hand-lettered in purple Magic Marker and rubber-cemented with scissor-cut crayon renderings of famous storybook characters, detailed the library's Saturday morning Mother and Child Story Time program.

It was six-thirty. Story Time was scheduled to begin in an hour. It warmed my heart to see programs like this being offered. I'd managed to save the binding and a few index pages of *The Egyptian Book of the Dead;* if I waited a bit, I could drop them off on my way home, then stay on at the library and witness this vital childcare service in action. I crossed the street and hid behind a car fitted with a wide-angle passenger-side rearview mirror perfectly angled for personal grooming. My hair was matted. I finger-combed it, using spit for styling. There wasn't much I could do without a proper bath. Saliva did at least remove a layer of thicker grit plastered like a fright mask on my face, but my nails were mechanic's nails, my arms the arms of a dirt farmer.

At seven, Rita Henderson, our volunteer head librarian, arrived in her Buick. She unlocked the library and went inside—my cue to tuck in my shirt and shuffle out of concealment. At first I was afraid to confront Rita. I loitered awhile in Young Adult. It's my business, after all, as an educator, to keep abreast of school-age literature. I have to say that I was shocked by the number of YA volumes dealing with death in one form or another: the loss of a sibling, a parent, a friend, a pet; cancer, addiction, war. And the fiction! Title after title featuring orphans.

"Why, Pete Robinson, is that you?"

"Oh, Rita, hi." Time to approach the checkout desk. I watched Rita raise her eyes to take in my face and arms splotchy with leaf and scum. I'd sustained scratches on my knees and ankles; dried blood discolored socks and shoes. What a mess. I felt that hot-under-the-collar tingle that accompanies lying to an authority figure, when I said, "Say there, Rita, I just had a little accident with a library book."

"Oh dear."

"Yeah, well, here it is," removing the destroyed tome from the knapsack and placing it gently on the counter. She stared at its sad dust jacket swaddling bent boards and unglued, water-bloated paper shreds. The spine was collapsed, ink was running—it was pathetic. I went on, "I was doing my morning mowing and hedge trimming, you know. I honestly have no idea how the book managed to get into those weeds."

"You defaced this with a hedge trimmer?"

"Mower, actually. Yes, it was, I believe, I'm sure in fact, the mower."

She gave me a look. "Hmn."

"A riding mower. That's why the damage is so bad. Those things have monster blades."

"Indeed."

Now other people filed into the library, mothers bringing their kids to Story Time. They looked me over and stopped. There was Sheila Moody with her son, Steven, a sensitive boy who'd attended kindergarten two years before. And there was little Susy Jordan, cradling in her baby-fat arms the same ragged plastic doll she'd toted through first grade. What a sweetheart. I called to Susy's mother, "Good morning, Jenny." And I said, "Hello, Steven. Hello, Susy. Hey, it's story time, isn't it?"

"Answer the man," Jenny Jordan instructed her daughter.

"Yes."

"And what is today's story?"

"Don't know."

"Today we've scheduled *The Legend of Pocahontas,*" Rita Henderson said.

"Ah. Our national lore. That's fine."

Rita told the mothers and children, "Mr. Robinson here has been having lawn troubles." Well, you could feel their skepticism. I grinned deliberately stupidly and exclaimed, "Ran over a library book. Riding mower. High gear. Couldn't stop. Sticks and rocks flying." Rita's apparent acceptance of my "lawn mower" con offered me comfort and strength; it served to integrate me with the larger community represented by these family groups. I milked the role of benign neighborhood duffer by boasting to the gathered throng, "I guess I'm not much good with lawn tools. Say, Rita, you wouldn't happen to have some hot coffee, would you?"

"We've got coffee and doughnuts in back. I'll bring some out. Don't you worry about this book. Accidents do happen. You're lucky you didn't lose a hand or a foot. Why don't you sit down and unwind a bit."

"Thanks, I'd like that." I watched moms and kids file into the Juvenile section. Juvenile is my favorite of all the special collections in the library. Along with, maybe, History. The Juvenile section is decorated with colorful, messy finger paintings and a collection of kids' Play-Doh statues of anthropomorphic beings, marbles stuck as eyes in their heads. Juvenile has its very own card catalogue and semicircular seating unit, one of those comfortable wraparound sofa environments, scaled down to youngster size and richly pillowed in stuffed animals: polar bears, kittens, multicolored birds, lions and tigers, an elephant, a bison. Beholding those kids hopping, now, into that playtime bestiary—it filled me with joy. I headed right on over and reclined among them, little Susy on my right, Steven and Brad to my left. Susy grabbed a python. Steven cuddled a bear. I got the bison. Other kids completed the circle, a boy named David and his redheaded infant brother, Tim; a puffy girl named Jane who looked like she'd been crying recently. Most were preschoolers. They all clutched animals and stared my way with wide gazes. One, an auburn-haired girl of, I guess, five or six, dressed in a floral-print jumper and saddle oxfords that wore friendly smiling schnauzers' faces sewn onto their uppers, said, "Hi, mister."

"Hi."

"Are you a monster?"

"Sarah!" her mother scolded from a folding chair beside the *World Books.* I said to the mother, "It's okay," and I asked Sarah, "Do I look like a monster?"

"Yes."

"I'm sorry," Sarah's mother said to me. To her daughter, in treacly, charm school cadences, she said, "Do not be a rude child."

I noticed Jenny Jordan blanching at the sound of this fierce other mom. I winked at Jenny (it was good to have an ally), then explained, patiently, "Sarah, there are two kinds of monsters. The real kind are scary and evil, and you always want to watch out for that kind of monster. Then there's another kind that's not a monster at all, just a person having a rough day."

"Like my dad?" Sarah asked. All I could do was chuckle, "Heh heh. Kids."

Luckily Rita arrived with refreshments. "How do you take your coffee, Mr. Robinson?"

"Black." I flipped the bison on its back and balanced my Styrofoam cup on its synthetic-hair tummy. Rita addressed the gathering, "Mr. Robinson is married to a mermaid, isn't that nice?"

"Oh," cried mothers.

"Well," I said.

"Now don't you be modest, Mr. Robinson. Meredith is a special person, and we're fortunate to have her in our town."

Rita took up an oversized volume emblazoned with four-color images of Native Americans enacting ceremonial violence. She held the book up to show a black-haired female helplessly watching a bare-chested chieftain sporting a feathered headband and hoisting a rock poised to descend onto the head of a trussed and bound white man. Rita pointed out, "This is Pocahontas, the beautiful Indian maiden, and this man with the rock is her father, Powhatan, and this man here is Captain Smith, the man Pocahontas secretly loves, and here is their story. Everybody ready?"

"Ready!" chorused the kids. What a sound. I only wished Meredith could've been present to hear that happy racket. Meredith was probably just waking up. I pictured my wife rising sleepily from bed and walking to the bathroom for her morning shower; I saw her brown hands rotating faucet knobs for hot but not too hot; I imagined her sudsing up, and felt blessed, there in that library resounding with cries of children, blessed for this woman of beauty and intelligence, sharing my life. I might, one day, earn political glory, and that would be fine. But she was an absolute gift, not to be undervalued. Her skin. Her hair. Her voice.

Rita Henderson read, "'Now Pocahontas was a very distinctive princess. Smart, pretty, and skilled at sports. Hers was a simple life. Forest creatures were her friends.'"

The pre-schoolers cradled their inanimate pets. I held my bison and stroked its downy ears. The image of Meredith in her shower rose up, rose up in my mind and in my heart, thrilling and pacifying me. Rita continued, "'One day, voyagers arrived in Pocahontas's land. Brave, strong men, sailing the ocean in ships.'"

She held up the book to show a watercolor of a fully rigged man-o-war flying the Union Jack and dancing over liquid seas. She turned the page and there was the same vessel with sails furled, anchored on a sunny topaz bay dotted with brightly painted bark canoes carrying warriors. A shoreline was partly visible: dunes, saw grass, a pine stand where sea-birds might nest. It looked peaceful.

Rita went on, " 'The Explorers brought many gifts with them, including books. Soon Pocahontas learned to read and write. And not only in English. Pocahontas was fluent in Latin, Greek, and French. In those days, people knew the classics.' "

This last bit couldn't've been actual storybook text. No, Rita was seizing an ad-lib opportunity to promote literacy. Well, why not? I watched little Sarah wag her head and kick her feet; her dog-faced oxford lace-ups rose and fell over the soft lip of the sofa seat. She was a cutie, Sarah. Reddish-brown hair curling neckward, round cherub cheeks, eyes the color of the painted water on which Rita's illustrated boat sat serenely moored: blue-green heartbreaker eyes. I know it isn't good to describe toddlers in adult sexual terms, but when you're around children as much as I am, it's hard not to think about them maturing. I pictured Sarah with long legs and a tan, and with wetness at the corners of her mouth, not from burping but from kissing.

Rita's voice interrupted this reverie. "Isn't that right, Mr. Robinson?"

"Excuse me?"

"I was pointing out the virtues of tolerance and respect between peoples from diverse walks of life."

"Right. Yes. Certainly." What was she getting at? Nothing. She was just being herself.

I sipped coffee. The bison's belly, where the cup had rested, was wet and warm. It felt sweet. The kids seemed to be enjoying Rita's spurious elaboration (appropriated, if memory serves, from the "children's classic" *Heidi,* in my opinion one of the world's more defective pedagogic texts, an inane paean to cruelty toward the physically disabled—disabled readers, that is, who *can't* get up from their wheelchairs and walk, like Clara—rationalized as Christian rectitude and saccharine good manners)—but anyway, as I was saying, the kids seemed to be enjoying Rita's elaboration of Pocahontas's daily hikes down the precipitous mountain path to read Virgil to her blind grandmother. I kept thinking about little auburn-haired Sarah—the "adult," not the child. This image was, of course, a modified Meredith. Sometimes, with my wife naked and pressed close to me, her breasts and stomach and the fronts of her legs on my chest and stomach, on my legs, well, we wouldn't even bother to pull away the strands of her hair coming between us into our mouths.

The tots on the sofa made curious gurgling noises. Occasionally one of the mothers would go, "Shhh." Rita read patiently through all these familial sounds. " 'For true love of her Captain, the girl did hazard her own dear life.' "

I bolted the dregs of my coffee. It so happens I know a thing or two about the Pocahontas legend, and the fact is there's convincing doubt in certain academic circles regarding the veracity of John Smith's "true biographical" account of his dramatic rescue at the hands of the daughter of the chief of the Chickahominy. Smith was a well-known self-aggrandizer and brownnoser who was suspected of embellishing his travel narratives (published to acclaim in London) in order to gain favor and influence at court. Still, it's a good tale: a sexy pagan throwing herself in death's way to deliver a Protestant. Why wreck things for a bunch of kids by invoking esoteric polemics? I set the soft white Styrofoam cup on the floor, stood and whispered, "Rita, thanks for everything. Sorry about that book. Give my best to Jerry."

She paused in her reading. "Why, Mr. Robinson, we're coming to the best part."

"I've really got to be going. Back to the lawn and all. No rest for the weary."

Rita said, "Children, can we all say bye-bye to Mr. Robinson?"

"Bye-bye," said the children.

"Bye-bye," I said back.

"Bye," chorused the moms.

"Bye," I said again. "Bye."

Then out the door and into morning. Right on Water and right again onto Wisteria, walking fast through humid air settling over tall palms that threw no shade over the tile roofs of neighborhoods where dogs barked. Out here in the world, things appeared normal. There was, and this seemed fitting, a distant somber growl of lawn mowers chewing grass. Difficult to say how many lawn mowers, or down which streets. Here and there insects darted, their luminescent wings brightly sunlit. A man fetched a paper from his sandbagged porch. I waved to him, and he kindly waved back. Farther down Wisteria, a girl wearing shorts and a halter top rode past on a bicycle, her hair trailing her. "Good morning," the barefoot girl cried.

When I arrived at the house Meredith was seated at the kitchen table, studying the morning edition, munching toast and drinking tea. She wore her indigo cotton bathrobe loosely belted; her hair hung wetly combed. I cruised over and stood by her chair and looked down the front of her robe. Floral scents of shampoo filled the air. Newspaper headlines splashed across the blue Formica table in front of my wife's belly: SPORTSMAN LANDS RECORD MARLIN, HUGE FISH CALLED "ASTONISHING." Breathlessly I said, "A minute ago I imagined you in the shower, and now here you are, you must've been showering at exactly the instant I had my vision."

"I thought you didn't believe in that kind of thing." She tilted her head back to gaze at my unshaved face. "Did you come to bed last night? Where were you? And what's that thing?"

She was referring to the bison, which I'd unthinkingly carted home, underarm like a football. I tossed it in the corner and told Meredith, "I'll explain later, let's make love," flinging away the knapsack, stripping off my shirt, running gritty hands over Meredith's arms and shoulders. I licked the back of Meredith's neck; I squeezed her; hugged her; reached down and pulled the sash girdling her robe.

"Pete, wait. We don't have time, Bob's coming over."

"Bob?"

"From the Holiday Inn yesterday. We made an appointment. He's going to help me reenter trance. Bob says it's crucial to stay with the initial impulse and follow the open stream to the unconscious. He's offered to coach me on breath work."

"What's that?"

"Rhythmic breathing required to induce feelings of emotional well-being. It's part of a safe and secure trance experience. I'm sorry, honey, I have to get dressed. We can have sex later, okay?"

"Can we?"

"Yes."

"Promise?"

"Yes."

But later Meredith went swimming feverishly into archaeology. It was ten o'clock on a bright new day. Sunlight poured into the living room, hurting my eyes. Bob, the trance coach, who was a pleasant-looking guy if you like a closely trimmed mustache wrapping a thin mouth—Bob reclined on our living room sofa and instructed, "In, out, in, out, easy, ride the feeling, yes, calm, right, deeply now, let it out slowly."

Meredith sat on the rug in half-lotus position. She wore summer clothes revealing shoulders and back, and, on her mouth, lipstick of an ephemeral cast. Now her eyes were closed, her tanned feet bare. I watched her toes twitch, and I noticed her head metronomically nodding in time with twitching toes, back and forth, back and forth; she looked opiated. I reclined a few feet from her, in the big wicker armchair. Bob had made me promise to keep quiet during the proceedings, a superfluous request, I thought, and one that was invasive, but what could I say? I slouched down low in the chair, propped my feet on the coffee table, drank my bitter coffee. I hadn't had a bath and my clothes smelled. Pounding drums rolled from stereo speakers flanking dusty bookshelves. Every now and then Meredith shuddered; her body stretched and jerked. It frightened me to watch this. Bob leaned away from her and toward me; his eyes were, I saw, very, very deep in his face. In low, confiding tones, the professor explained, "We're witnessing a personal devolution from lung to gill breathing. It's a process of psychic regression in which the trance initiate accesses memory at the cellular level and rides the DNA chain like a wave back into prehistory."

"Ah."

Meredith's mouth opened and closed; she made gulping noises; her body swayed. The more this went on, the more it depressed me. Midmorning sun kept blasting through the living room windows onto my contorting wife, whose movements seemed to me, within the context of Bob's presence, indecent. It was a question of marital intimacy and the sanctity of environment: namely, this room, stocked with furnishings selected by me and Meredith, together, for our life.

Bob leaned forward on the sofa. His face hovered close to Meredith's. He tapped one foot in time with the drums. The scent of flowers filled the air—a bowl of drying rose petals rested on the shelf above the records Meredith and I used to play while we made love on the sofa in the days before we could afford a proper bed. Meredith's dress was hiked up and from the right angle you could see up it, and this made me anxious because I couldn't tell whether Bob was getting a view. He wore a vacant gaze. Meredith performed little irregular motions, making her hair fall forward over her face to cover her eyes and mouth. I reached out to adjust her clothes. It was hot in the living room and everyone was sweating. Meredith's head rested on a pillow embroidered with images of fish. Bob's voice intoned, "Deeper, Mer," and she twitched.

I could've left, and maybe should've. I could've gone upstairs and gotten undressed and stood awhile in a hot shower, then toweled off and shaved and brushed my teeth and, perhaps, if I'd felt the patience for it, flossed. Or I could've gone downstairs to the basement and tinkered with my miniature dungeon. There was no end of fine painting to do, delicate detailing with a fine artist's brush. I had plans to refine the rack installation in minor yet significant ways—realizing detail of a different kind, structural, using balsa or one of the rich tropical hardwoods: gumbo-limbo or—if the mood struck and my X-acto blades were sharp enough to get a good cut—softer, malleable mango; and also I had lately been mentally dramaturging possibilities for figures to occupy the scene: a hooded Inquisitor fashioned from a refigured toy soldier, gesticulating and ranting articles of faith while brandishing an illuminated manuscript before a martyr T-pinned to a Styrofoam wall.

Needless to say, I didn't descend to the basement. I didn't leave my sweetheart's side.

I put down my cup of cold coffee, closed my eyes, and listened to Bob say, "Venture into darkness. Open your inner eyes. Gaze into the mental whorl . . ."

In and out I breathed. My heart was pounding and my head was heavy. I wanted Meredith in the worst way.

"Prepare to dive!" the voice of the anthropology professor commanded.

Followed by: "Find your animal!"

What happened after that is something I'd rather not go into. Not right now at any rate.

It's too painful, too embarrassing.

Anyway, I have town meeting minutes to type. I believe I mentioned these earlier—all that business of voluntary mine sweeps of Turtle Pond Park, funding for the library, etc. It's my duty as Town Scrivener to record and type such official civic business of the body politic.

Why did I ever volunteer for this distasteful service? The answer is simple: to burnish my public image. Certainly I hold no ambition for secretarial tasks. Which goes a long way toward explaining—though I realize it's hardly an excuse—it goes a long way, this clear lack of enthusiasm for the mediocre in life, toward explaining why I'm so far behind on the minutes. I should've filed them ages ago.

Maybe in a while I'll come back to that Saturday morning with Meredith and Bob in the living room. However, now I need a breather, and work, I've found, is the only true way to forget pain and sorrow.

The minutes here on my desk offer a challenge. Not only are they hastily handwritten, they're also smeared—the ink is smeared in blurry, psychedelic patterns. Some fool must've accidentally placed a water or beer glass on the paper. I may have to fudge the illegible passages. Also, many pages are torn, which is in a way fitting considering that this is an account of a wild night. I refer of course to the big town meeting at Terry Heinemann's Clam Castle, out at the end of Fountain Lane where Fountain dead-ends into the municipal beach parking lot.

Everything started innocently. It was Saturday night, the

night after my burial expedition with the foot. Other pieces of Jim waited at home in the freezer. I felt weary and frantic about life. The Clam Castle was crowded with taxpayers: Jerry, Bill, Abe, Tom, Robert, Betsy, Dick, and many other business professionals including several of my old teaching colleagues: Alan, Simone, Doug; and all the spouses, too, along with a few children old enough to be trusted to stay quiet during open discussion; and Meredith's mother, Helen, who hated the status quo and was apt to be vociferous; and, of course, Terry, whose generous all-you-can-eat-for-one-special-low-price deal was the reason we were convened at the Clam Castle in the first place. Terry went from table to table, jotting down orders for cherrystones on the half shell, clam rolls, sodas and coffee. On the slate for that night's meeting: the above-mentioned topics (domestic conflict in Turtle Pond Park, the dying library system—what to do), plus various proposals for licensing and regulating construction of pits, moats, mounds, craters, furrows, ditches, channels, trenches, follies, bastions, breakwaters, balustrades, barricades, battlements, bulwarks, and all other acropolis-like structural additions to private houses, garages, and utility sheds in residential areas. It was only a short time, a couple of weeks, since the death of the ex-mayor, and though no one in town was talking much about Jim Kunkel, at least not publicly, not out loud, well, the spirit of the man, his memory, hung heavy in the seafoody air.

I had a plate of cherrystones. Meredith stood over by the unplugged jukebox, which hulked like a dead thing. She looked lovely leaning against its massive flanks, chatting with her mother. Helen Mooney was dressed in a lemon-yellow pants suit; she wore her steel-wool hair in a bun. The mother seemed so small next to the daughter. I clicked my ballpoint and spread my notepad on the big wooden picnic table covered in red-checked vinyl. The restaurant lights, imitation "harborside" gas globes, burned low, but there were candles on the tables, gentle candlelight lighting my notebook pages and the faces of my table companions: Jerry, Rita, Barbara Nixon. Barbara looked unhappy and sexy, the latter quality due to the slinky manner in which her clothes fell off her shoulders, presenting superb tan lines. She dined, as did Rita, on seafood salad. Terry's Clam Castle seafood salads are pretty good, not just lettuce and a couple of boiled shrimp. I was beginning to wonder if I maybe should've gotten a seafood salad myself, instead of the cherrystones, which don't go far. I looked around to place an order with Terry, or with Claire, Terry's aloof, angry waitress, and I saw Meredith waving to me, and I waved back; but when Meredith continued to wave I realized she wasn't waving to me at all, she was welcoming Bob, just arrived and securing a seat at the table next to mine, Bill Nixon's table. Why were Bill and Barbara not sitting together? Were they fighting? Nixon had a plate of clams like mine. I watched him squeeze a lemon over it—the whole lemon, not just a wedge. Abraham de Leon's voice boomed jovially from over near the men's room. What would Abe be dining on tonight? The whole menu, probably. Jerry, next to me, was halfway through a clam roll. Jerry's clam roll looked and smelled delicious, and I decided that this, the clam roll drenched in tartar sauce, would, if I could only flag Terry or Claire, constitute my next order.

Jerry crunched and swallowed a deep-fried morsel. He

slurped some coffee, then rose to his feet and addressed the crowd: "Okay, people, let's come to order."

The room gradually got quiet. Jerry said, "We have many articles of interest before us. I suggest we skip the formalities and proceed straight to business."

"Second," called Tom.

"All in favor say aye."

"Aye," came the group response. "Nays?" queried Jerry. The floor was silent. Jerry continued, "The chair will now entertain motions," at which point Tom Thompson rose from his seat at the bar and said, "I believe tonight's topics are in many ways interrelated, and so propose that they be discussed concurrently, as one issue, rather than separately."

"Hmn," said Jerry. There was a period of thoughtful murmuring about this idea. It was a fine point requiring subtlety of mind to appreciate, and therefore surprising, coming from Tom. Jerry, apparently aiming to avoid complexity, declared, "The chair appreciates the speaker's motion and takes it under advisement for future deliberation. Yes, in the back there?"—referring to a red-haired woman wearing a nurse's uniform. She was Mary Brown, a staffer at the hospital emergency room, and a divorced mother of two. Mary Brown stood and read from a legal pad, "I represent a group of mothers who have signed a petition"—waving her pad—"calling for action in the matter of these moats and trenches and et cetera, so popular of late in the community. Not only are such additions to property unsightly, they pose certain danger to children and pets. Allow me to read a partial inventory of pit-related injuries treated during the last month at Anhinga Memorial. Harley Geer, aged seven, extensive cuts about the legs, arms, and face when he chased a ball into a neighboring lawn ringed by a ditch filled with broken window glass. Sheila Wells, aged fourteen, near loss of a foot after stumbling into a big hole full of steel animal traps, many rusted. Drew Smith, aged sixteen—"

"Uh, I think we get the picture. In light of the fact that there are a number of children present, I suggest we forgo further itemization of specific cases." Jerry's gaze swept the room. What a smooth tactical move on the chairman's part: by interrupting on behalf of childhood innocence, Henderson co-opted the hospital worker's position, undermining it and making the petitioner seem strident.

Leave it to Meredith's mother to take issue. "Point of order. Let the speaker finish. Put it to a vote," Helen Mooney commanded from her post near the jukebox.

Jerry sighed theatrically. "We have a motion on the floor. Do I hear a second?"

"Second," called a woman I couldn't see. I leaned toward Barbara Nixon and whispered, "Who was that?" Barbara shrugged, "Beats me," and Jerry blared, "All in favor of hearing, in the presence of minors, the speaker's full catalogue of injury and impairment, say aye."

"Aye," muttered a few irresolute voices.

"Nays?"

The nays swamped the ayes by a large margin. Mary Brown clutched her legal pad tightly, pressed it to her breast, as Henderson said, "Please, do carry on." There was nothing for the healthcare worker to do but flip yellow pages and forage for a new beginning: "Well, anyway, we have this petition and we'd like to see actions taken in the way of bylaws because clearly these pits are unsafe and who knows anyway why anyone needs them or why anybody in their right mind . . ." She ambled on awhile; she sounded, actually, near tears. I glanced toward Meredith and her mother. Both looked my way with disapproving faces. What did they want me to do? I just kept the minutes.

When the nurse was done Jerry wrapped up. "Thank you so much for that illuminating and thoughtful viewpoint. The floor will now hear an opinion from Mr. William Nixon."

Chair legs scraped floorboards. I turned to see Bill towering above his plate of barren clamshells. Bill wasn't much of an orator, but this didn't matter because he embraced a solidly anti-intellectual style; his grass roots positions always won him a popular following. Today Bill kicked off, "The other night I was out sitting on the porch with my family, taking pleasure in the twilight sounds of birdsong. Well, what do you think we heard off there in the distance? High-caliber semiautomatic rifle fire is what. You know it's that kind of a rapid cracking echo, like plinking but mixed with a coughing sound at the same time? My six-year-old Jeff said, 'Daddy, are those AK-47s or M-16s?' "

He paused for a sip of water. What would it be like to be this guy's kid? Dismal. Nixon was undoubtedly a stern disciplinarian. To be his child would be to endure intolerance in the guise of paternal charity. Bill cleared his throat and embarked on a protracted screed about target marksmanship, home ownership, the joys of gardening, and the Rule of Law. It wasn't particularly coherent stuff. Or maybe it's just my minutes that don't make sense to me—Bill's inflammatory town meeting speech is all but lost on one of those pages defaced by a water or soda glass. I guess I might've set my iced tea down on the notes without realizing it. After all I wasn't, I'll admit, paying especially close attention to Nixon. I was watching his wife, Barbara. I was, in fact, having a hard time keeping my eyes off her. I do not believe it was purely a sexual thing. Bill ranted, "I don't want some animal lover telling me to put up a chain-link fence around my lawn-based defense cavity because he or she is afraid his or her dog or cat is going to run in there." He chuckled at, I guess, this ironic image of a fenced-in trench or moat. Several men and women in the audience chuckled along. Bill puffed out his chest and finished, "Friends, little Jeff's home with the sitter tonight, and let me tell you I feel a whole lot better knowing there's a network of electronically triggered fragmentation bombs armed and ready in the nasturtiums outside his window."

Thunderous applause, followed by Meredith's mother's reedy voice hollering to challenge Bill, red-faced and beaming and gesturing expansively with his hand in the air, gesturing to Claire smoking a cigarette at her waitress station adjacent to the service bar. It was a little drama: Bill waving at Claire, Claire exhaling smoke in a vertical stream past her upper lip, Bill waving again, Claire grinding her cigarette butt into one of Terry's trademark clamshell ashtrays, and so on like that. Finally Claire gave in, grabbed her order pad, and ambled toward Nixon's table, as, from the region of the jukebox, Helen Mooney's voice trumpeted over the hooting of Bill's supporters, "What exactly are you afraid of, Mr. Nixon?"

Well, you could hear a pin drop. I snuck a glance at Bill staring Helen's way with his squinty eyes. It was a face-off. Nixon inhaled a wheezy breath. He leaned forward with his hands resting flatly on the tabletop, and said, "I'm not afraid of anything."

"The hell."

"Listen, I'm not sure what's bugging you. If you have something to say I'm ready to hear it."

"Are you?"

"Don't be playing games here, we're here to do town business, this is town business we're doing here!" Bill's face was a mask of red stress. You could see him struggling to contain his emotions. Meredith's mother, on the other hand, retained her composure; she stood with arms crossed and head tilted to one side; she looked like the home economics teacher she had once been, thoughtfully appraising a child with an attitude problem. Meredith looked my way and rolled her eyes. How I loved her for that!—the bond of shared irony. I lowered my gaze and pretended to be busy scribbling minutes. Barbara Nixon peered down too, not acknowledging the antagonists; she dug around with her fork in her salad. After a moment she noticed me noticing her, and she put down her fork.

Then Claire was beside Bill's table, flipping through her pea-green check pad. Claire held aloft her pencil and, in a voice kind and soft with waitressly forbearance, inquired, "Yes?"

It was Bob, not Bill, who answered. The anthropologist pointed to his open menu and said, "I'll have the fish chowder dinner and a side order of hush puppies, please, and, um, a draft."

Which gave Jerry an opportunity to move the meeting along by proclaiming to the room, "I think it might be wise to consider Tom Thompson's earlier words about the interconnectedness of things, and in this spirit propose we move on to the problem of the library system. I now call on our volunteer librarian, Rita Henderson."

"Thanks, hon. The situation is this. Current levels of funding prohibit comprehensive acquisition, and outreach programs like Story Time and the bookmobile will probably have to be discontinued. I've developed a plan to merge the neighborhood branches into our main, Southshore location. Redundant editions can be sold to raise money for one of those magnetic checkout devices, which I think we should have one of."

"No doubt," said Jerry, who proceeded to motion for a committee to assist his wife. Hands flew up and I scribbled down nominations: Barbara Nixon; Betsy Isaac; Simone, the art teacher (who'd get my vote any day); Ray Conover, obviously not present; and Chuck Webster, likewise absent; along with a host of other likely and unlikely candidates, including, of all people, Abraham de Leon, who nominated himself. Jerry grimaced when Abe raised his hand and said, "Me." Was something up, after all, between Abe and Rita Henderson, and did Jerry maybe know or suspect? Or was the chairman merely appalled—and who could blame him?—by his buddy's clear lack of diplomacy in throwing his own hat into the ring? Whatever the case, Abe wasn't anyone you wanted overseeing any libraries.

Jerry motioned to close the floor to further nominations. Though not before Helen Mooney raised her hand and declared, "I nominate my daughter."

"Second," many people shouted.

So it was that Meredith came to be part of a select commission authorized to engineer social programs and allocate funds. She won more votes than any other candidate. I wasn't jealous, exactly. After all, I already held a civic post. Though mine was, of course, voluntary, not elected. I felt, well, strange—a mild case of territorial anxiety mixed with healthy domestic competitiveness. Also, I was proud of Meredith's new popularity. What can be said about that? A lot of folks were enthralled by her ability to become a fish.

Other worthies elected to the task force were Simone, Barbara, and, as luck would have it, Abe, who bellowed, "All right!" when his name was called.

"Order," demanded the chair. I still hadn't managed to get myself a clam roll, which was probably a good thing because another plate on the table would've made it very difficult to write minutes. I turned to a clean notebook page and scrawled down Jerry's call for "ten-minute recess, after which we'll reconvene to discuss interfamilial strife and also, if time allows, the matter of a multipurpose public school / indoor sports complex to be located at Freedom Field and headmastered by our own Mr. Scrivener."

Down came Jerry's gavel on the tabletop. Down plummeted my mood with it. What a rude turn of events. When had I consented to this? I turned to address Henderson but he was already up and gone. I spotted him leaning over the bar with a gaggle of town hall types. Was it time for the drinking to begin? Already? I heard Rita shout, "Could I please see the library task force over by the ice machine?"

I sat alone. Across the room Barbara and Meredith embraced, gently patting one another on shoulder and back, like chums or sweethearts—teammates! Barbara said something and Meredith laughed. Rita orbited Abe like a minor planet. Abe looked like a biker—if it weren't for that golf shirt. Beyond de Leon: the sea, faintly, blackly visible through a decorative "porthole" installed near the men's room door.

"Well, Pete Robinson."

It was my mother-in-law. I rose, and, because form dictated it, we hugged. Helen's bristly hair tickled my face, and I thought I might sneeze, when she said, "How wonderful, a new school. I've always found it so gratifying that my daughter should choose a husband who values education."

"Our children are our future."

"Indeed they are. Tell me, son-in-law, do you anticipate a traditional curriculum?"

"Uh, could be. Too early to tell. Lots of problems to be worked out and all."

"It's high time we got back to solid values of fundamental learning and common human decency."

"I agree."

"Do you? Do you? I believe evil has found a home in your heart, Pete."

Before I could say, Excuse me? Tom Thompson came over and smiled. "Hi guys."

At which point I finally sneezed, not once but serially, causing nearby people to pause in their conversations and take turns saying, "God bless you, God bless you."

I have to admit, I kind of like Tom. His politics are unsophisticated but his heart's in the right place.

Take his speech, once recess was over and the meeting resumed: "The Bensons and Websters are waging private war on public land!"

"That's right, that's the issue exactly," observed assenting voices. Tom was well known for his enthusiasm. Crowds excite him. That night at Terry's he gave a memorable performance, stepping into the center of the room and holding aloft his arms and claiming, "I for one am prepared to make a nonviolent gesture of protest and self-sacrifice. Who'll join me on a walking tour of the park to locate and deactivate those mines?"

No hands went up. Jerry said, "Noble gesture, Tom, but I don't think it's that simple." I sneezed again. "You're catching a little bug, aren't you?" whispered Barbara, and I felt her breath on my ear. Wow. I imagined the feeling of her mouth, its warmth. And I saw an opportunity to integrate a lot of issues into one action; I blew my nose into an oversized paper napkin, folded the napkin into a pocketable square, pocketed it, and said, "Okay. A Turtle Pond Park initiative is desirable. I deem it appropriate to take decisive action in the form of removing obstacles to enjoyment of the park, and suggest an alternative to walking through it, thus risking grave injury. What if Rita's soon-to-be-redundant large-format library reference editions were simply hurled into park grounds? The *World Book, Columbia,* and *Britannica* encyclopedias could possess the heft required to depress the claymore's trigger."

After that things got out of hand. Why, I ask, should a mere suggestion incite divisive bickering leading to vehement altercation? A simple no vote is all that's required, not yelling things like "You're crazy, Pete Robinson, you don't give a damn about education!" which was what Helen shouted at me, repeatedly, so that finally Bill Nixon got fed up and went steamrolling unsteadily across the room—nearly flattening a child who was roaming innocently between tables with a milk-filled jelly glass that wound up inverted—getting right up in her, Helen's, face. Granted, Bill's tactic of swatting at Meredith's mother like a fly was imprudent. He didn't appear to intend actual harm. The mother of the milk-doused child shrieked, "That man hurt my baby!" Which wasn't true, because, after all, it was only milk. Blood did not flow until Abe, presumably resolved to uphold the peace, imposed himself between Helen and Bill. Abe counseled his friend, "Take it easy, chief." Too late. Abe's nose got whacked by Bill's hand. It's a good thing there was a nurse in the house.

And there was Meredith. The crowd parted to let her through. She stood bathed in Terry Heinemann's Clam Castle's amber mood lighting, cautioning, "Boys, boys."

It was a thing to see, the way everyone fell quiet and turned to look at her. Even the little children stopped their crying.

Meredith offered Abe a napkin, then gave her right hand to the person on her right, her left to the person on her left. She said, "Let's all join hands for a minute."

Well, everyone did. It was kind of a chore for me, holding Jerry's hand, but this was more than made up for by Barbara's cool palm pressing mine. Meredith said, "Why don't we go outside and breathe the night air."

In the parking lot we all formed a large circle. People I knew held hands with people I didn't: an unbroken chain beneath the Big Dipper. Light winds carried sweet ocean salt on a mist that rose from slow waves breaking against the jetty. Lifeguard stands loomed. In the harbor: moored day sailors equipped with aluminum masts and homemade cannon, clinking with tackle and line, making bell sounds; and the deeper, melancholy pitch of the distant bell buoy, rocking beneath the moon.

"Look at the moon," said Meredith. We looked. It hovered yellow and large above the sea. Yellow moonlight skipped off white sand and turned the flickering wave tips silver-gold. Looking farther out, the eye followed a shining highway of moonlight traveling over deep water to the horizon. Meredith said, "The light of the moon makes a shining path to each of us. Wherever we stand, the path will cross the water to find us. Go up or down the beach, and it will follow."

"Yes," said people in the circle. And, "That's right." In this way, a vision we'd seen and taken for granted all our lives, simple reflected light, became miraculous.

Later, after the meeting was over and everyone had gone home, Meredith said to me, "Let's go out on the jetty and take off our clothes, like we used to. Want to?"

How I did. How I wanted to get naked on the rocks with my moonlit wife. But I have to report that after what had happened that morning in the living room with her and Bob and the sound of drums rolling from the stereo, I didn't think the jetty was anywhere I wanted to go.

What happened was this. It was midmorning. I'd endured a sleepless, ghoulish night in the rain. The foot was buried, I was bushed, and my coffee was cold. I mean, I was out of it, slouching in the big wicker chair and watching Meredith sway to the drumbeats and Bob's cadenced breathing instructions:

"Easy, easy, slow, slow."

Meredith's eyes were closed. Her dress hung loosely about her legs and hips. I leaned forward to adjust the fabric. She inhaled and exhaled. I watched her toes twitch, and I noticed her head nodding; and my head nodded too, in time with hers, when the trance coach commanded, "Prepare to dive!"

Suddenly I was weightless. Everything felt still and cool. I drifted in the wicker chair. The voice of the professor told us to find our animals, and I looked up to see a silvery fish with boxy jaws and round eyes fixed to oblong sides of an enormous head.

The living room was gone. It was a world of blue. The big fish showed lustrous teeth. One great fish eye stared at me. We were face-to-face. I opened my mouth and bubbles came out when I inquired, "Honey, is that you?"

The fish's gills flowered open to catch the current—I took this breathy fluttering for a yes. Sideways swam Meredith the coelacanth; I watched her corpulent torpedo length rotate into view, fins fanning. Then the gills lightly closed against translucent pink flesh and the white of bones dimly visible. No bright shafts of sun streamed downward to illuminate these obscure depths; only a vague semiglow lit that oceanic darkness full of beings and things: my primordial, buoyant wife; midnight configurations of rock and reef behind her; and my own hands, icy cold and floating weightless to reach out and caress Meredith's beautiful metallic face, which I wanted to kiss even in spite of those scaly lips. Perhaps she, too, felt the gravity of attraction: she flexed her body, bared her gills, wiggled her tail, darted minutely forward to perform close-in pecking motions—as if feeding! Her heavy snout nipped my nose, but gently. Such strange pleasure. I paddled toward that divine fish face. "Let's fuck now," I called to the pretty young thing with the impressive teeth. She did a little flip. I reached out to stroke her spiny erect dorsal fin, which I gamely imagined might bear erotic as well as hydrodynamic utility. That's when I noticed that my hands were no longer hands, they were hooves. Fur wreathed them. They galloped and stamped, kicking sand and sending bottom life scurrying for the low cover of the reef. Overhead the love of my life swam around and around; her watchful lidless gaze did not leave me; nor did I ever look away from her, as the change came over me and I became my animal and knew myself to be a bison.

For her part, Meredith wore a wild look. The problem was that I was in the wrong ecological habitat and was dying. Loamy mud sucked me down into itself, as an abundance of matted brown buffalo fur rose kelplike from my own mammoth breast, filling my mouth and washing up into my burning eyes. All I could see was nothing. Love and dread fired my beating heart, and I cried, "Meredith!" but no intelligible sound came out, only hoarse bellowing through the brine.

For a while I fought. Then there was nothing to do. I breathed in the cold. Closed my eyes. Felt Meredith's cool lips on mine.

All the pain went away, and my frightened mind became silent and blue.

Sometime later I opened my eyes. I was in the living room, flat on my back, looking up at the ceiling. Bob's face floated into focus. The assistant professor was sitting over my hips in the sexual posture of someone giving a backrub, though it was my front and not my back getting the rubbing. Close by was Meredith. She wasn't a fish. She was on her knees, her body rising above me. Beyond her: eggshell walls and ceiling showing plainly visible cracks spiderwebbing from stained corners, a hairline map of creeping water damage reaching almost to ceiling's center. Was the roof leaking?

Bob's hands pushed on my sternum, pushed me down into carpet sponging beneath me. On my skin: a coating of prickly warm sweat. I felt Meredith's hand reaching out to touch me, the forefinger and thumb pinching shut my nose. She leaned over me and lowered her head. Her face, seen like that, by which I mean from below, coming down—her face looked like the face of someone preparing to drink directly from a stream, as watched from beneath the water's surface. Here came Meredith's mouth opening to show tongue and teeth. Here came lips. I tasted lipstick, felt Meredith's hair feathering down to tickle my forehead and neck, when she pressed her mouth against mine.

"Breathe," Bob commanded, as air from my wife's body flooded me. For a while it went like this: he thrusting rhythmically down; she blowing; he letting up; she raising her head to take in fresh oxygen before descending again in search of the seal between our mouths. Finally I lifted my hand from the floor and touched the back of Meredith's head, as if guiding her to me.

She took a long breath and said, "Phew."

"We experienced a convergence," said Bob, climbing off me, now, to sit cross-legged on the floor by my feet. "Once in a graduate seminar a guy became an amoeba and accidentally parasitically invaded his girlfriend's GI tract. She had to go on antibiotics to get him out of her system."

A joke? Some kind of academic drollery? Bob trying to put us all at our ease?

Meredith, cradling my head in her lap, told me, "I saw you down there, Pete. You became a magnificent Great Plains bison. You almost kicked me in the face."

"Sorry."

"It's okay. You were drowning." She stroked my head. It was good to feel her fingers roving over the scalp, tracing idle patterns through the unwashed tangle of hair. Sunlight came in every window, and the air smelled of orange blossoms. The drum cassette had long since spooled itself out. It was Saturday and I was alive.

"How about lunch, everybody?" Meredith said.

"Sounds all right to me," replied Bob.

Meredith's hands abandoned my head, and Bob helped me up. We made our way—Meredith leading, followed by Bob, then me, feebly—into the sunny kitchen. There was a brief moment of fear when Meredith, leaning over the freezer chest, digging around, in fact, inside the freezer chest, sorting packages, said, "Honey, where's that chowder I made a while back?" But then she found it, and soon we were seated before misting bowls of potatoes, celery, and clams in a subtle cream broth. Meredith sat on my right and Bob sat on my left; we formed a triangle lit by natural light. Meredith and I hunched forward over our places, not yet eating. Rather, we paid close attention as the anthropologist explained the morning's accidental near drowning:

"You didn't have firmly established boundaries, Pete. The

dominant animal inside you came right up and occupied your undefended mind. This is great chowder, Meredith. Do you make your stock from scratch?"

"Yes."

"It's wonderful"—crumbling, into his wide china bowl, a cracker; spooning up a white crusty spoonful—"perhaps you'll grant me your recipe. Unless, that is, it's a treasured family secret."

"I'd be delighted to give you the recipe."

"I'd love to have it. I mean that. Anyway, Pete, you're high and dry and that's what matters. Right, Meredith?"

"Right."

"I have to say, if you don't mind my saying so"—and here Bob helped himself to another vast bite before turning to regard me with that hollow stare of his (what was this guy's animal? Gila monster?)—"you're one lucky hombre, Pete."

"Thanks." But for what? Having Meredith to be married to? Being alive? I inquired of Bob, "Dominant animal?"

"An animistic persona construct expressed as an embodied archetype. We all contain this. Yours regrettably found itself enmeshed in Meredith's cerebrocabalistic sphere."

He turned his gaze on Meredith. Boldly, unashamedly, he looked her up and down. After a minute he declared, "Yes, she is carrying a lot of power."

What was there to say to this? Anything would be wrong. I lowered my head to watch my spoon stir up a rotary wake in the cooling broth—I was playing with my food. I felt deficient. My insides were ulcerous from coffee and terror. How was I supposed to eat? What was needed was a lengthy session on the can. Listening to Bob offer tribute to my wife—

"Truly, Meredith, I am being one hundred percent honest when I inform you that never, never before have I witnessed, within this or any other culture, a keener mastery of the cataleptic condition and its psychic imperatives"—listening to this and watching Meredith nod and smile and say, "Really?"—it made me feel like I was being killed by a knife.

I guess I'd have to say that, all things considered, it's not surprising in the least that the town meeting minutes I took by candlelight later that evening at Terry Heinemann's Clam Castle came out, for the most part, illegible.

Or that Meredith's suggestion about getting naked on the jetty, all slippery and wet above the crashing ocean waves, made me nervous.

"No thanks," I told her. It was late. The municipal beach was deserted, the night was dark. Jerry and Rita Henderson, and Abe and Tom and the Nixons, and Terry and Claire, everybody, had gone home. Who knew what time it was. Meredith stood on soft sand beside me. I felt overwhelmed by sadness and the conviction that I had failed in some impressive way. By not becoming a coelacanth. By not *being* a coelacanth. Wasn't our relationship (marriage) founded on care and the veneration of intimacy and fidelity? Hadn't I violated this? What could be worse, in a close sexual relationship, than showing yourself to be a different species than your mate?

"We're really different," I said, in tranquil, rising tones intended to suggest the beneficial aspects, whatever they might be, marriagewise, of biological diversity.

"Hmn."

"Well, I guess it's not so bad." What nonsense.

We stood staring at waves rolling in, and at the distant

black water shaping the horizon. On any other night I might've asked Meredith, "What are you thinking?" Tonight this seemed an ominous line of inquiry, particularly with what felt like acute hydrophobia coming over me—I had to turn away from the breaking waves and concentrate on the yellow streetlamps hanging like bleached moons over the Clam Castle parking lot. Our purple Toyota glowed brown beneath their light. Other cars, in varying shades also tinted a gaseous brown, were parked far away, but no people were around. Only those cars washed in lamplight, and the dark restaurant, and a green Dumpster that gaped open, spilling fishy trash.

It was well past bedtime. Most good people were in their homes, making love or sleeping, washing dishes or listening to music or getting up to check on a sick child, reading, talking on the phone, drinking. We were just kicking sand, my honey and I.

"Want to go?" I said, and we walked to the car. We drove home past booby-trapped houses shrouded in fan-shaped leaves and gray hanging mosses. I was thinking, as I guided the car along the spooky streets, of children. It seemed to me that Meredith, silent beside me, might also be thinking about children.

That night we cuddled in bed, but it was melancholy cuddling. I wasn't sure what part of her to touch. I rested my hand on her hip, she slept curled in a ball.

A few days later I set out, alone, on foot, to comb the neighborhood for likely recruits for the home school.

The day was overcast. A gray impenetrable ceiling of sky seemed hammered to the tops of tall trees and the roofs of houses. Campaign slogans came to mind: PUT THINGS IN PERSPECTIVE WITH PETE. A VOTE FOR ROBINSON IS A VOTE FOR SANITY. GOOD OVER EVIL, THE ROBINSON WAY. That's the great thing about politics: success rests in unashamed immodesty. Which is not, in and of itself, a bad thing. These particular campaign poster slogans spoke to the morbid depression I'd been feeling lately. Was it inordinately grandiose to assume a general public despair, on a cheerless day like today?

My first scheduled stop was Dave and Jenny Jordan's, over on East Manatee. Other houses with children were closer, but Jenny Jordan had seemed so sympathetic and kind, that morning in the library during Mother and Child Story Time. It was probably wise to pitch the school to a friendly listener before taking this act to strangers. Also, little Susy Jordan was the perfect age for the school, right around seven or eight. If I could enroll Susy, who was widely known to be bright and talented, I could then drop her name with the parents of other children, as a draw.

The Jordans' modest wood-frame home, fifth on the right past the intersection of East Manatee and Fountain, sits only a short distance, about a block, from Jerry and Rita's moat-enhanced corner-lot villa. Walking past the Hendersons', I kept careful watch for serpents. What exactly did I expect to see? Vipers bellying forth from watery nests to slay hapless pedestrians? No, your moccasin is a docile creature, unless disturbed at home. The waters in Jerry's moat sat brown and still. The drawbridge was up, everything seemed peaceful. For fun I threw a rock. The splash sent ripples against the poured-concrete banks of the moat, but nothing happened as a result, and so I continued on down the somber lane bordered in diminutive purple wildflowers. Along the way I checked the shrubs and flower patches for a viable burial site for Jim's liver, which seemed an appropriate follow-up to the foot, seeing as it was an organ and therefore rich in multicultural symbolic properties of an altogether different order than hand or foot (by which reasoning the genitals, being both organ *and* extremity, would come, naturally, last in the interment procession); and also because the liver was so big, considering its origin inside a little old bald guy, and thus quite easily detectable by Meredith, down in its hiding place beneath the restaurant-sized bag of fish sticks, deep at the icy heart of the freezer chest.

Interesting to note, here on Manatee—not one of the wealthier lanes in town, though by no means poor, either. Solid middle class—interesting to note was the pride of workmanship apparent in the various domestic fortifications. These were well-planned, sturdy structures, erected by gifted home-improvement enthusiasts willing to lay out for topflight materials. Case in point: Dan Gleason's ingenious "Rainbow Pillbox" at 23 East Manatee. Gleason, who works, or did until recently, at the local boat basin, spraying fiberglass onto the hulls of recreational vessels, had used this same industrial aerosol technology to apply a white lacquer of composite slipperiness to his house, transforming it into a fantastic hump-backed windowless bunker with a nautical screw hatch for a door. The roof, a low dome, had ganged at its apex a cluster of heavy-duty latex garden hoses, spewing forth. The water cascaded out of the hoses, over the roof, down the hard-shell walls, and into PVC runoff gutters sunk neatly into the flower beds. This spilling sheet of wetness gave the entire house a strategic "banana peel" unscalability, rather like an omnidirectional theme-park water slide. The water also served as an excellent exterior surface coolant for the house, reducing Dan's air-conditioning bills, one would imagine, by a considerable sum. A sump pump recycled the flow. Sometimes, in early morning and late afternoon, sunlight playing on the translucent building caused rich, shimmering rainbows to appear, as if painted on the walls.

Nobody'd seen Dan or his family for a long time. Presumably they were happily ensconced and doing okay. The lawn looked recently trimmed; water was running as usual over the rooftop; everything seemed fine. I proceeded past the Rainbow Pillbox, past Bob and Linda Hamilton's amusingly named, two-bedroom "Beaver Dam," and after that, Ed and Jane Shapiro's "Fort Ed and Jane" (not such a finished job, Fort Ed and Jane—an eyesore actually, resembling nothing so much as a complex split-level plywood clubhouse hammered together by stoned teenagers), arriving, finally, at 57 Manatee, the home of the Jordans. This was a house that was still, to the naked eye, a house. Which gave me pause. I stood for a moment on the sidewalk, peering at the grass and the small bushes lining the driveway, searching, among the ubiquitous purple flowers, for what if anything might befall me upon setting foot off public, onto private, property. But there was nothing out of the ordinary here, only porch furniture parked up on the porch, and a couple of toy trucks and other children's play objects littering the walkway. I stepped over one truck. Then another. At the foot of the steps rested a Big Wheel. I breathed out the tension before gripping the Day-Glo plastic trike and rolling it gently from my path. And at the door, rather than thumbing the buzzer, which could be hot-wired for electric shock, I knocked.

"Hello?" The voice of Jenny, calling from deep inside the house. I heard her approaching footsteps, and hollered back, brightly:

"It's me, Pete! Pete Robinson? From the library the other day?"

"Oh, hi," opening wide the door, gesturing me into a living room crowded with matching furniture and more kids' toys, and smelling like a hamper. "You'll have to excuse me, the house is a mess. I've got the kids all day and there's only so much a person can do."

She wore that haggard young-mother look. Messy blond hair, bare feet, a wrinkled blue sundress hanging from bony shoulders. Susy, her seven-year-old, peered from around a hallway corner. I waved to her and said, "Hi there, bet you don't recognize me with a shower and a shave."

Susy made a face. Her mother asked her, "Pumpkin, did you finish your cereal?"

"No." Followed by: "Yes."

"Go finish."

"Okay," vanishing, with the refreshing sound of small feet. I complimented Jenny, "Great kid."

"Isn't she? We have a lot of fun, me and Susy. Brad's around here somewhere too. He's still kind of in the labor-intensive phase."

"How old is Brad?"

"Going on five. You want to sit down? Watch out for that stuff on the sofa. It's part of Brad's Erector Set."

I picked up the debris in question, a constructivist replica of what appeared to be a mobile missile launcher, complete with retractable blast shield, tractor wheels, the works. "Brad built this?" It seemed incredible. Jenny explained, "With help from his sister."

"Ah."

"Do you, Mr. Robinson, have children of your own?" She smoothed her dress in her lap and leaned forward, attentive. Her naked feet, pressed side by side on the floor, were narrow and smooth, and showed strong arch support and excellent toes.

"Meredith and I have decided to wait. We're both teachers, so, you know, it isn't like we don't get to enjoy the company of children."

"It's so terrible about the schools." At that moment there was a great crash in the back of the house. Jenny jumped up, called, "Sweetie?" and jogged down the hall.

Her absence gave me a chance to peruse the bookshelf. The usual assortment of paperback classics, plus a surprising amount of hardcover new fiction. Not many people buy hardcovers these days. I pulled down a few volumes, then put them back as Jenny came in, smiling. "Would you like a cup of tea, Mr. Robinson? Why don't we go in the kitchen where I can watch the monsters."

"Call me Pete," following her into the warm kitchen that smelled of a mixture of foods; smelled also, like everything in this house, of the children, just now visible through the screen door, out back naked and splashing each other in a small blue inflatable pool shaded by a tree bearing round fruit. Brad was blond and fat, Susy dark and thin. Their mother held a kettle beneath the faucet. "Unfortunately, my drain is clogged. You don't know anything about clogged drains, do you, Pete?"

"Hmn. Did you try chemicals?"

"I poured Drāno down there but that stuff worries me. You're not supposed to use too much, but how much is too much? Linda Hamilton down the street used Drāno and it ate through the pipes."

"Their drain's clogged too?"

"Yup."

So it *was* a community problem. How widespread? And what could be causing it? "Do you have a snake?"

"A snake?"

"It's a thing that bores through the drain, to dislodge whatever's in there. A long metal thing, but pliable. My drain was clogged, and I used a snake."

"Your drain was clogged?"

"Yes."

"Recently?"

"A few days ago."

"Weird."

We peered together into her sink drain, I over her shoulder, gazing down. It was the closest I'd ever come, I think, since I'd gotten married, the closest I'd come to pressing myself, front to back, against a woman not Meredith. A smell of soap rose from Jenny's freckled neck. The small hairs behind her ears were quite appealing. We stood there, breathing. Kids splashed, sink water stood. The kettle whistle blew and I backed off into the middle of the room as Jenny, in a voice hard to read, a little sharp, a bit curt, said, "Don't worry about it. Dave will take care of it when he gets home."

"When does Dave get home?" What a stupid thing to say. It sounded like a line. But it wasn't a line. Not entirely. "I mean, what kind of work does Dave do?"

"Junior administrator at the junior college."

"You guys wouldn't happen to know a visiting anthropology professor named Bob, would you?"

"Bob Barrow?"

"Skinny guy, deep-set eyes."

"Sure, we know Bob."

I sipped tea. What was the right tack? Were Barrow and the Jordans friends? Or did Dave's business bring the Jordans routinely into contact with faculty, in which case it mightn't be personal. Test the waters.

"He seems like a nice person."

"Bob's brilliant. His theories about intracranial cross-speciation are groundbreaking. But the psych research community is very hostile to people like Bob. He poses a threat. That's why he's guest-lecturing at the jaycee, and not holding an endowed university chair."

The splashing of the children was becoming intense. Dripping faucet water plinked in the sink basin. We sat at the kitchen table. I spread my legs and leaned back. Jenny held her teacup at chin level, near her face, giving herself a miniature steam facial. We talked about this and that. Jenny's breasts showed beneath the fabric of her dress. She had graceful arms and slender hands. What kind of animal might she be? Ocelot? Sea otter? Certainly not a ruminant. Her breath blew steam from the top of her cup. I maintained an expansive lounging posture of alpha male insouciance, keeping my distance while subtly displaying, in the language of the body, mild assertiveness, a sexual openness. And I allowed my feet to come close to hers beneath the table—I was sure Jenny was aware of them by her chair. Her elbows rested on the table, her face floated. Her voice was mellow and inviting. "Well, Mr. Robinson, I mean Pete, what brings you on this visit?"

"School."

"School?"

"Grades K through six, starting next week, at my place." I put down my cup and leaned forward, facing Jenny across the table. We were inches from one another. I told her everything about the school except the political part, the "junior achiever" mayoral-campaign strategy. Also, I didn't mention Freedom Field. My plan was to avoid that thorny subject altogether. I spoke freely on topics like moral guidance, A. S. Neill and alternative education, the Jeffersonian concept of the honor system, box lunches, and so on. It was a pretty speech, lasting about ten minutes, which was a pleasant surprise to me, seeing as I'd neither planned nor rehearsed. I wrapped up, "Jenny, let me assure you, it's going to be amazing."

"What's this going to run?"

"Tuition will be enrollment-dependent. We're looking to offer top-dollar education at economy rates. That means special emphasis on each child's distinctive needs, within a friendly, traditional, family-style setting. That's the home school advantage."

"Susy! Brad! Come in here!" Suddenly the two sopping pink children ran howling from pool to porch to kitchen; the screen door slammed and daughter and son stamped in, streaming water. They stopped and stood in the dirty puddles they made, before us.

Jenny leaned over to address them at eye level, "Susy, Brad, what are you supposed to do before you come in the house after swimming?"

"Um, dry?" This from Susy, assuredly the leader, by virtue of age and intelligence, of the sibling pair. She clasped her brother's arm and began tugging him roughly back toward the screen door.

"Hang on," called her mother.

Without letting go of Brad, Susy turned, her quick and forceful motion requiring Brad to race around her in a half-circle, like a cruelly led dance partner. He almost slipped and fell. Jenny scolded, "Brad, be careful, the floor's wet. That's why you're supposed to towel off."

Susy said, "I've got him, Mom. I won't let him fall." It was one of those beautiful family moments, the elder child's urge to nurture and protect.

"Guys, this man wants to be your teacher. How do you feel about that?"

I couldn't believe it. Was Jenny going to leave the education of her children, aged five and seven, in *their own hands?* The kids watched me with blank expressions. Susy seemed to be squeezing down on Brad's arm—she was giving him an Indian burn. I smiled benignly, winked in a charming, avuncular, fun/conspiratorial way, generally nodded and grinned, as Jenny pressed her offspring, "What do you think? Want to study with Mr. Robinson?"

It was all about trust. I was being judged. By babes. It hadn't occurred to me that I might have to win over the kids.

But of course that's always the way. Parents seem to embrace, almost unquestioningly, this bizarre, superstitious belief in infant clairvoyance, as though their "innocent" offspring have access to deep truths lost to them, to the parents—lost to maturity, cynicism, compromise. It's one of our most esteemed cultural archetypes: the Prescient Child.

Brad and Susy didn't strike me as a couple of oracles. In fact, they looked a little stupid. Even Susy looked stupid. Her mouth hung open, her hair stood up in wet spikes. I wanted to come to her defense, to hers and to Brad's, to say to their mother, Don't lay this on them, it has to be your choice, you're their mother.

But then Susy spoke, in syllables soft and quiet, too quiet, almost, to be heard. "Okay."

It was sweet, I could've hugged her. The home school was now officially in business. Enrollment, two.

"What will you call your school, Mr. Robinson?"

Good question. "We'll see when we get farther along. A school is a place to make sober inquiry into the workings of the world and the mind. The name of the school, the right name, should reveal itself through this inquiry."

Robinson Country Day? The Robinson Academy of Arts and Letters? The Robinson Institute? It was, after all, my idea, my ideology. It was *my* school, in *my* house.

I made a total of seven recruitment visits that day and the next, was successful at each, and in danger of dying only once, when Deborah and Carl Harris's automatic garage door/catapult discharged a fusillade of calcified coral fragments, missing my head by inches.

Deborah Harris cooed apologies from the house, "Yoo-hoo,

Pete, sorry about that. I *told* Carl to turn that thing off. He must've forgotten."

"I'm fine," rising from the Harrises' lawn and brushing myself off. "That's quite a device."

"Hey, Pete." It was Carl Harris, emerging from the dark garage with a crescent wrench in his hand. This man had once spent twenty days adrift on the high seas in a rubber raft, with no fresh water, surviving on the blood and flesh of fish caught bare-handed. LOST PLEASURE BOATER LIVES! ORDEAL CALLED "HARROWING," ran the headline. Looking at Carl now, you wouldn't guess such a thing possible. His skin was white, he had a gut; he ambled splayfooted on short, bowed-out legs. "Almost plugged you, Pete. I've been experimenting with a new garage-door-to-air gyroscope."

We shook hands, and I said, not discourteously, "I guess it's a good thing you're still experimenting."

"Hell, Pete. I had no idea you were out there. Please believe me. Please, accept my apologies."

"Apologies accepted. It's my fault, too. We've all got to be more careful these days."

After that it was easy to get Deborah and Carl to commit their ten-year-old twin sons, Matt and Larry, to the school. I felt no remorse about playing on the Harrises' contrition—they *had* almost killed me. Besides, the important thing was the education of the children. "Okay. School starts next Monday at eight. We haven't worked out busing, so for now it'll be the responsibility of parents to provide transportation to and from, and also you'll need to supply Matt and Larry's lunches. I recommend a sandwich, Pop-Tarts, and a piece of fruit. You might stock up on eight-ounce cartons of low-fat milk. Additionally, we ask all students to bring along a favorite toy. I typically kick off the year with an open play session, in order to implant the idea that learning is fun."

Deborah said, "The boys' favorite toys are their bow-and-arrow sets. Is that going to be all right in class?"

"What kind of arrows? Do they have metal points, or those rubber suction cups?"

"They're carbon steel shafts with two-bladed broadheads and helical fletches. They'll shave a hair," said Carl.

"Tell you what. Have Matt and Larry bring their bows and quivers, and we'll work out something in the way of a target range out back."

Which is exactly what we did, come Sunday—we affixed, Meredith and I, to the tangerine tree out back, a round piece of cardboard painted eggshell-white and crayoned with an imperfectly round, lavender bull's-eye. I held the flimsy target against the trunk and queried, "Higher? Lower?"

"Higher."

"Here?"

"Up more."

"Here?"

"*Higher.*" She came and held the target against the tree while I delicately tapped in narrow finishing brads meant for fiberboard or plaster, for hanging light pictures. I'd gotten the nails from the tool cabinet in the basement. They were short, soft, inadequate.

"Pete, can we talk? About those fifth- and sixth-grade bio electives I was going to teach? Seeing as, so far, there aren't any fifth- or sixth-graders? I mean, there's Susy Jordan, she's smart enough for bio, she's smart enough for physics I'll bet, but you know, she's only second grade. I thought I might take the opportunity to switch over from science, and do an elective in religion."

"Religion?" It seemed like trouble, tackling religion at the elementary level, though what kind of trouble, and for whom, I wasn't sure. Meanwhile the nails were bending; it was as if they were made of putty.

"Pete, I feel like I don't know anymore what's up and what's down. It might help me to teach a course in spiritual doubt," biting her lower lip, brushing away from her face, with one hand, a hovering green bug. Meredith's abrupt movement shook free a couple of imperfectly pounded nails, which trembled from their ragged holes and dropped to the ground. No way this crummy cardboard bull's-eye was going to withstand arrow impact. I chucked the remaining picture nails and Frisbeed the cardboard over the pit; it winged spinning in an upward arc, planing skyward, six, eight, ten feet. In higher air it paused—the illusion of rest at the peak of ascent—before plunging to rest atop a triangle of nautical spear tips.

"Touchy."

"Sorry."

"What's bugging you, Pete?"

I clutched the hammer. The sun was directly overhead and the air cool. There was a distant sound of splashing water—the Kinsey kids, no doubt, performing elaborate nose dives, cannonballs and can openers and watermelons and such, in their shallow aboveground vinyl pool. This mid-afternoon country club clamor of pre-adolescent recreation reminded me to take a stroll around the block and pay a courtesy visit to Delia and Hiram Kinsey, who most likely would voice no objection to sending their kids to school by way of a couple of backyards, provided right of passage could be obtained from the McElroys, which might be difficult considering Pat McElroy's staunch isolationism, a position echoed all too clearly in the menacing advertisements posted on trees and the picket fence wrapping the McElroys' quarter-acre lot: BACK OFF.

"Karen Kinsey is twelve. That's sixth grade exactly," I told Meredith matter-of-factly.

"What are you saying? I should hold bio lab for one pupil? You know, Pete, I'm having a hard time getting on board with this whole school idea. I know you want to help. I believe you want to do the right thing as a teacher. I believe you believe in education. But I don't get it. Here we are out in the yard tacking up a bow-and-arrow target on a tree, and there's a hole full of stakes three feet away, and I guess I don't get it."

"What's to get? Archery as a phys-ed elective? Come on, it'll be great. The target range is well away from the trench. Look, I'll show you," dropping the hammer and walking to pit's edge and bending down, carefully, kneeling in the soft muck, one hand on the ground for balance, the other reaching over the tops of Meredith's pretty bamboo spears (a narwhal and an inverted "pop art" snow cone cup), in order to retrieve the fallen target; and, target in hand, pacing off steps, toe to heel to toe, from pit to tree. "Right. The target range isn't *three* feet, as you say, from the pit, it's, well, let's see here, it's about, what? Seven? I fail to see the problem."

"Seems dangerous is all."

"Kids, Meredith. Kids. What are they going to do? And if you or I come out here and coach safe shooting, that's a plus, as I see it."

"How so?"

"Proper coaching inspires respect for weaponry and helps define the concept of sport."

"Why do you think you have to do everything, Pete? This isn't our responsibility. Other people's children, Pete. They're not our children! They're not our responsibility!"

Such exquisite distress. But what, exactly, about? Was I being condescending? Was I lecturing? It's a problem of mine, I'll admit it, a tendency to become insistent to the point of excluding other people's viewpoints. It's something a lot of teachers probably struggle with in their personal lives: the adamant vocal style appropriate for driving home a lesson, and yet so hurtful among friends or at home.

Meredith shook her head and gave me a look it seemed best, in the spirit of marital harmony and academic diplomacy, to overlook. I said, "Do you suppose we might get a spare set of encyclopedias and dictionaries from one of the libraries? Hon?"

"I can check with Rita, but I think all the oversized volumes already went to Abe."

"Abe?"

"He and Jerry and the other guys liked your idea of throwing books at the land mines in the park. They loaded up Abe's van this morning. I forgot to tell you. They're over there now."

"At the park?"

There was no time to waste. I grabbed wallet and keys and hopped in the car and fastened my seat belt and backed out of the drive and sped off hurriedly through moderate downtown shopping traffic. On Water Street I got nothing but green lights all the way to Hyacinth; it was as if God were clearing a path. Explosions sounded from the direction of the park, dull concussive rumbles like construction site dynamite, audibly and subaudibly vibrating the hard and elastic surfaces of things: steering wheel, gas pedal, the car seat headrest, my head. Along the way, on Main Street, I noticed a bright sign in the window of Dick Morton's clothing store, BIG WEEKEND CLEARANCE SALE! ALL MENSWEAR HALF PRICE! EVERYTHING MUST GO! and I made a mental note to stop in there later, to see about purchasing some presentable new dress shirts and a snappy bow tie to start off the teaching year.

At the park, things looked wild and dark. There is, of course, no auto access to the grounds, so I pulled up on the street outside, right behind Abe de Leon's Dodge van and Tom Thompson's Mazda. I shut off the engine, got out and locked the car door, then walked along the sidewalk, searching for a gap in the bushes, a route into the hammock. Everything was quiet, not even birds called. Presumably all the forest creatures were tensed up, waiting for bombs to go off. Overhead, twisted hardwoods draped leaf-heavy branches over thickets of briar and thorn that clogged the park's walkways and nature trails, strangling smaller botanicals and forming a natural barrier between the roadway and the interior. It was impossible to see more than a few feet into that savage foliage. Finally I plunged on in, stepping lightly, pausing occasionally to orient myself, and to remove thorns snagging my clothes, brittle green points anchoring in the fabric's weave, biting through to draw blood. Was Ben Webster still combing these woods for his vanished father? Or had son and dad reunited and gone home to a hot meal and comfortable beds? And Ray!—it grieved me to imagine a smart, personable guy like Conover, running berserk in swampy public hammocks, rending his clothes.

Too bad I hadn't brought along Jim's liver. This was just the place for it. The liver filters bodily impurities, it's a giant sieve, a living trap for waste and virulent matter. These bushes growing everywhere, blocking passage, making headway into the park arduous and painful, were malignant floral impurities, invading and infesting a once pristine family recreation spot. Gone were the sun-dappled company picnics and barbecues, the Frisbee tosses and touch football matches. Now vigilantes gathered here to detonate explosive charges, using literature. And wasn't this, in a broad cultural sense, impure behavior? In which case, mightn't the ritual burial of a liver—and it needn't even be buried, it could be unwrapped and tossed frozen into a patch of weeds, as a figurative, multipurpose cultural antitoxin/herbicide—mightn't throwing Jim's liver into the bushes act as a corrective to the strife and neglect that had lately transformed this serene leisure space into a grotto of death?

"Pete!"

It was Abe himself, hollering from the deep cover of a mountainous shrub:

"Duck!"

From the skies it came, a gargantuan blue tome, one of those Compact Editions of the *Oxford English Dictionary,* end over end hurtling in projectile descent, pages fluttering and tearing in the wind, a screaming index of printed and bound lexical data, half a language heavy with gravity and gathering velocity. I dove for turf and covered my head as the *OED* cruised thumping to the earth.

When I opened my eyes I saw that it was the P–Z volume. A–O was lying nearby, loose pages from it papering the ground. The Supplement text was nowhere to be seen. Buried in some leaves? Already blown apart? Waiting, still, to be launched?

Here came the men. First Abe, followed by Bill Nixon and Tom Thompson and, taking up the rear, Jerry. They walked single file, like a ghastly family of four on an outing. They wore identical radiant orange hunting caps and Day-Glo pack vests over camouflage safari shirts. Each sported a hand-tied white armband that appeared to have been ripped from a bedsheet. Sure enough, Tom carried the *OED,* Supplement. He also wore a backpack. Bill, true to form, clutched a beer can in one hand, and in the other—this not at all typical of the man—a *Webster's.*

"Hi, guys," followed by handshakes all around:

"Pete."

"Tom."

"Teach, how're you doing?"

"Okay, Bill. You?"

"Fair enough."

"Hello, Jerry."

"Mr. Scrivener, good to see you."

"You too. How's Rita?"

"Rita's doing fine."

"Say hi for me."

"Will do."

"Hi, Abe."

"Almost clocked you there, Pete." Abe offered me a strip of white sheeting. "Put this around your arm. It identifies you as a neutral party."

I tied on the armband as Jerry explained the procedure: "Okay, first one of us throws his book, and the others try to get theirs close to that one, like in horseshoes. We want to saturate any area where a mine might be planted. We cover some territory, collect the books, and move on in a straight line. Slow and safe, no one gets hurt. Got it?"

I wasn't sure I did. "Yeah, sure."

Abe, crouching among the scattered A–O pages of the *OED,* shoveling up a thick handful of unglued papers, said to Tom, "Tom, my man, this one's shot."

Tom lowered his pack, reached inside, and brought out a *Crowell's Handbook of Classical Mythology.* He handed it to Abe and reached in again, this time bringing out a *Roget's Thesaurus,* which he offered my way. "Pete?"

"I could use another brew," Bill said.

These, as well, were in the backpack. I took the *Roget's Thesaurus* from Tom, who dispensed a round of semicold ones. In unison we pulled back our pop tabs, a chorus of fizzing metallic clicks echoing like strange insects in the birdless forest silence. We raised our cans to our mouths and drank. The beer tasted wonderful to me, numbing my throat and warming my heart. Abe said, "Why don't you give that thesaurus the heave-ho, Pete."

"Me?"

"Show us your arm."

"It's not much of an arm, I'm afraid."

"Send it over there, Pete," suggested Bill, gesturing vaguely with his beer can.

Was this something I could reasonably do? Throw a book at potential oblivion? I know it had been my idea, I was responsible for all this. But I never actually believed, back at the Clam Castle town meeting, that anything like it would ever come to pass. It was one of those ideas designed to lead to a modified version of itself. Ideally we'd be hurling something like those miniature bowling balls found at certain lanes, the kind of ball you hold in your palm. These books were valuable. Maybe not the *Roget's*. I generally warn the kids away from the thesaurus because I believe they become reliant on it, when they should be working to build their own vocabularies through memorization. The *Roget's Thesaurus* could, in all fairness, go.

"Where?" I inquired.

"Wherever," answered Bill, raising and spreading his arms in a grand gesture of encompassment, taking in the world. He was crocked. He crumpled his can in his meaty hand and dropped it to the forest floor, then went immediately for another in Tom's backpack as Jerry, ever the diplomat, added, "We were headed south toward the gazebo. How about over by that big old oak, Pete."

I wasn't sure I could pitch a thesaurus, even an abridged version, which this was, all the way to the oak tree.

"Hold it like this," said Abe. The tall, bearded tax consultant clasped his *Crowell's Handbook* by the boards, fingers spread for good grip, palm over page fronts rather than the spine. "If you grip it by the spine it'll come open and you'll get a lot of drag." Abe feinted back and raised his arm, cocking for the throw like a pro quarterback; he let fly and the volume spun upward without opening or fluttering, the literary equivalent of a perfect spiral. As if on cue, we all hunkered down, backs to the possible blast. But the *Handbook of Classical Mythology* landed without event in a patch of wildflowers twenty yards away.

My turn. Abe's toss would be hard to beat. I faded back, set my feet, and let go with everything I had. The thesaurus flapped open, caught wind, and dropped like a shot bird. Ten yards.

"Nice try, Pete. You'll get the hang of it." Jerry smiled encouragement, pitched his book. The real estate developer threw sidearm, a modified discus-style spin toss using a full-revolution windup, complete with manly grunt at the instant of release, sending the great blue lexicon a surprisingly long way—short of Abe's, but not by much—thumping dully into the weeds. Next up was Tom, also hurling sidearm, though minus Jerry's grace. It was clear who'd been on the track squad. Still, Tom's *OED* Supplement toss was respectable, particularly compared to Bill's overhand *Birds of Prey Illustrated* "fastball pitch," which rocketed wild and crashed into a clump of aloe plants. "Fuck," Nixon said as Abe came up and made it look so very easy, lofting another of his beautiful play-action "long ball" heaves into the trees. Then it was my turn again, this time with a bound volume of a year's worth of experimental sociology abstracts. The abstracts were incredibly heavy. I said, "Tom, may I?" and fished around in the backpack for something lighter and not so fat, coming up, after much testing of bulks and widths, with *Biological Aspects of Mental Disorder.* There were many books in Tom's backpack, and one by one we delivered them all into the dirt and the grass, each time exclaiming things like "Looking good, looking good," or "Too high, too high," before ducking and bracing for the thud of an explosion. Between tosses Jerry filled me in on the direct-hit detonations back around the boathouse, the various types of trees and shrubs decimated, radii and depths of crater holes, pages flying like parade confetti. One blast, Jerry claimed—and this was verified by the others—one blast left a perfect, minute, cannonball aperture in the center of *The Darwin Reader*.

Now no explosion came. We tiptoed to our torn books, gathered them up, and threw again.

Later, at the gazebo, we reclined on cast-iron deck chairs and sipped the last of the beers. The chairs were straight and hard as church pews, arranged in a permanent circle, legs bolted into metal plates sunk into the wide gray floorboards. I sat facing Tom, with Jerry to my right and Bill and Abe to my left. An assortment of recently thrown books (the last no-hit salvo at the gazebo steps), and the backpack bearing more books and the beers, rested in the center of the circle, near our feet, within easy reach. The gazebo was an open, airy octagon, built of whitewashed wood and roofed in copper, and decked out in cornice-level gingerbread that threw intricate shadow patterns over the floor and our bodies. Past Tom's head I could see untended lawn bordered by tall pines draped in crawlers and epiphytes that bloomed lavender and white. A cracked plaster birdbath was entirely overgrown, consumed by creeping vines. And bugs were everywhere, getting in our faces, hovering and landing on sticky metal surfaces of empty, set-aside beer cans.

"I do enjoy the way *The Riverside Shakespeare* rides the wind on a long toss," sighed Tom.

"*The Riverside Shakespeare* does seem to float," agreed Abe, taking a swig from his beer. What kind of animal would Abe be? Something furbearing and immense and ferocious, obviously, yet with the potential for softness, and a warmhearted, friendly aspect: a walrus, a bear.

Bill said, "For hang time, give me *The Poetry of Robert Frost* any day." No telling about this guy. Bill Nixon could be any number of species of diverse phyla. Today he wore a sagging, unhappy face. Slouching in his gazebo chair, clutching his nth beer, he looked fungal.

Jerry swatted at a bee—several were circling in the air above our heads. Tom said, "Hey, Jerry, don't piss them off, okay?" and got up and placed his beer can on the floor a few feet away. He called out, "Here, bees. Here, bees." Sure enough, the bees descended, buzzing and congregating on the can's silver metal lip.

"Good thinking, Tom," said Jerry. Then: "You want to know what book I liked?"

"What?" asked Tom.

"Borderline Conditions and Pathological Narcissism."

"The Kernberg?"

"Yes."

We all drank, as if following a toast. Jerry elaborated: "I prefer a clothbound book with thin pages sewn in muslin to a medium-width spine. Anything with a lot of plates is going to be a problem. Art books for instance. You pitch one of those museum catalogues and you feel like your shoulder's going to come out of the socket."

"It's the varnished pages," Tom said.

I concurred. "They are a bitch."

Was it a weakness, my facile desire to go along with the guys at the expense of the books? Or was it more complex, a sincere inclination to favor present human company, fellowship and community, over the obscure pleasures of printed narratives? Certainly the air was cool at this time of evening. A wail of birdsong ascended from the gray-green trees. The men's voices were deep, the world seemed good, there were plenty of unimpaired books left lying on the floor and in the backpack. What did it matter *which* books? The essence of culture is found in all its artifacts.

With this in mind I surreptitiously took inventory of the assorted tattered volumes tumbled beside my chair. Pleasing to note were a quantity of university press editions, which would've been prohibitively expensive, new. One book, Thieleman J. van Braght's hard-to-find classic of Anabaptist distress, *The Bloody Theater or Martyrs Mirror of the Defenseless Christians Who Baptised Only Upon Confession of Faith, and Who Suffered and Died for the Testimony of Jesus, Their Savior, From the Time of Christ to the Year A.D. 1660,* struck me as an ideal gift for Meredith. It would show my love for her, by demonstrating enthusiasm for her commitment to religion and the spiritual life of children.

Martyrs Mirror is a big book, eleven hundred plus double-columned pages of "eyewitness" and court-record accounts of severe bodily torments, punishments, and executions, encyclopedically detailed and chronologically arranged, many accompanied by engraved plates illustrating dramatic scenes like "Vitalus Buried Alive at Ravenna," "Phocas Put to Death in a Lime Kiln," "Two Young Girls Led to Execution," and the poignant, closely observed "Georg Wanger in the Dungeon"—this last depicting the figure of a Christian (middle-aged, male, forlorn) reclining on a bed of straw. Gloom descends. In the etching's foreground a pair of largish toads seem to gaze reverentially up at the martyr-to-be, while near his feet, one of which is rudely chained to a wall, a viper coils to strike. Looming contours framing the illustration's lower quadrant may be mere rubbish, but they may also be skeletons and/or corpses. What a scene. It never occurred to me to include reptiles in my own dungeon. But of course. It made so much sense. What fun I'd have later, down in the basement, roughing out plans for a few 1:32-scale "bathsoap" bog denizens.

"You're one sick fuck, Pete." It was Nixon, leaning forward to examine the hefty volume open on my lap. He chuckled, a menacing, beery chuckle. "Heh heh."

"True scholarship knows neither health nor infirmity, Bill, only esteem for the heritage of man, and fearlessness before the misery in all our hearts."

That shut him up. Jerry said, "Pete, I take it you refer to the dark side of human nature. Is 'misery' the word you want to use?"

"Maybe not, Jer. Maybe just 'pain.' "

"How about, um, 'despondency'?" suggested Tom.

" 'Heartache,' " Abe said.

" 'Anguish,' " added Jerry. Which earned a "Hmn" from Bill, who contributed, " 'Rage.' "

We all thought about that for a minute, about rage. Jerry observed, "Good insight, Bill." Both Tom and Abe nodded their heads in agreement with this, smiling and saying, in near unison and with genuine if slightly sodden enthusiasm, "Yeah, definitely."

Which seemed to serve as a point of closure. It was that point during polite conversation when talk must either cease or become intimate, self-revelatory, deep . . . our cue to rise and begin gathering our things. Tom said, "Put the empties in the backpack, guys. I'll take them home and saw them up for my pit. That is, if no one else wants them."

The other guys shook their heads no, and I said, "Hey, why don't I help out by taking these library books."

Abe asked me, "What do you want with a pile of dusty old books, Pete?"

"Nothing. A little night table reading."

"That stuff? Before *bed*?" Jerry meant, I guess, *Martyrs Mirror*.

Bill said, "Barbara and I often enjoy thrillers before turning out the lights."

"Well, Bill," I said, commencing stacking—dictionaries and *Martyrs Mirror* on the bottom, miscellaneous professional-level science and psychology texts in the middle, a few soiled paperbacks on top—"Well, Bill, reading of any kind is better than no reading at all."

Of course I left behind the thesaurus, which I honestly consider pernicious.

Evening, and the park's dense thickets of trees and bushes seemed washed in eerie, nighttime shades. About that landscape one could truly claim: It was a jungle. Now off we went, single file down the gazebo steps, into it. The books in my arms rode heavy, towered head-high; I was forced to gaze around them in order to see the back of the man in front of me, Bill's back. In front of Bill, Abe and Jerry pushed through the weeds. Tom walked far out in front—point man. The trust-and-estates lawyer was visible as the red fabric of his backpack, audible as the sound of beer cans clinking softly, musically inside the pack, and as a gentle voice drifting back down the line, man to man, issuing safety commands: "Step high," or "Easy over these rocks," or "Let's go left around these wood lilies, okay?" Meanwhile the precious books shifted and slid between one another, their dark and light spines touching my face, bumping my face. Small dry kisses on the nose, and my arms aching from the cumbersome weight of paper. A few paces ahead, Bill lumbered through thorny briars that snapped back in his wake to slap or drag across the backs of my hands—a painful, localized flogging. Consider the martyrs. Here was my punishment: a hundred herbal lashes across the wrists and forearms for delivering literature out of the wilderness. How exciting, this difficult passage toward hearth and home. How I ached, along the long walk, for Meredith's touch. Desire came, a dull electric hum situated low in the belly, giving me the beginnings of an erection. Or perhaps this was merely the result of the steady, jostling pressure against my groin of all the weighty books. The configurations of the erotic are many and varied, and who can deny the arousing and, might I add, altogether requisite function of narrative in sexual fantasy. I imagined us sprawled together, my fish wife and I, open-mouthed and fucking in lovely harmony atop a sea of books, some scattered open (I'd offer to recline on the books myself, to protect Meredith from the sharp corners of the bindings), their pages damp and turned to vital texts describing the orgiastic death wails of the burned, the impaled, the drowned, and the flayed. I couldn't wait to get back to the house, to show Meredith my wounds and let her tenderly apply ointment and gauze bandages while I recounted the events of this brave day with the town fathers, The Day of Much Blood and Pain, and the Saving of the Schoolbooks. It gave me a nice idea for a mayoral-campaign slogan: PETE ROBINSON BLEEDS FOR YOUR CHILDREN'S FUTURE. I made a mental note to scribble this gem down when I got home, so as not to forget it once my hands were healed and no longer hurting.

Sad to say, the comforts of domestic life would have to wait. For when Tom Thompson finally called out, jubilantly, "Guys, we made it, we made it, here's the road," I heard also, at my back, another voice, a familiar, boyish whisper rising softly on the breeze that bore salty ocean scents over the tortured land.

"Mr. Robinson."

It was, in fact, my former pupil Ben Webster. So, he was still out roaming the gloom. I turned back briefly in the direction of the youngster's voice, but the tyro guerrilla was nowhere to be seen. He'd sounded so close. Clearly Ben had become adept in the techniques of jungle subterfuge. What a fast learner. It made me proud.

I whispered into the trees, "Ben, wait here for me," then turned and headed out to the road and our cars and a round of hearty farewells to Jerry, Abe, Tom, and Bill. Abe offered again to cart the books back to the library, seeing as he had the van and all. He was quite adamant, he kept at it, "Sure you don't want me to drop those off? I've got the van. I'm going that way anyway. No trouble for me. Really, no trouble.

Sure? Sure?" Finally Jerry snapped, "Abe, let Pete take the fucking books." There was, for a moment, between the two friends, some tension; it was a miniature alpha male, beta male face-off, though in this case with no readily distinguishable beta. Jerry tends to lead the pack, but Abe is of substantial build, he's physically intimidating, always a factor in these kinds of contests. Watching the two men glare at one another across the roof of Tom's metallic Mazda, it occurred to me that perhaps Abe's offer to return the books, his insistence in the matter, was actually cover for a visit—a tryst, even—with Jerry's wife, Rita, and that, at some level, Jerry knew or suspected his friend's mantled intent.

Bill stepped up to the Mazda and tamed the beasts by saying, "Hey, guys, come on, let's go over to Sandpiper's," which is the name of a happy hour bar on South Main. It was pretty clear that the man had a problem with alcohol. None of his buddies seemed to notice or be bothered by this. They all answered Bill's suggestion for continued drinking with hearty cheer: "Yeah, yeah," "First round's on me," "Okay, let's go for it." Most likely, Bill's friends misunderstood his heavy intake as a function of choice and disposition, of personal style rather than compulsion. Poor Bill. And poor Barbara. No wonder she always looked beat. Was she a drinker? Or merely suffering the ravages of marriage to one?

"You guys go ahead."

One by one the men climbed into their vehicles and fired up engines, destroying the silence of falling night. I watched their ruby taillights grow dim along the narrow road to Main Street. At last the cars disappeared. Quiet returned. It was that eerie time of night when the air becomes calm and the birds settle down and the world seems timeless. I dumped the books in the Toyota, wiped my bleeding hands on my pants, and sauntered back to the woods.

A few feet inside the fringe of trees Ben greeted me. It's amazing how much a person's appearance can change in a week. The former A student seemed to have dropped twenty pounds, aged a good twenty years. His bony, unclean face was the face of an urchin, his eyes were fugitive's eyes. Scrubby adolescent beard tinted jaundiced cheeks black; ripped clothes told of scrambling pursuits through the park's untended greenery. Ben wore his gun belt low over the hip, in the rakish style of a movie-matinee quick-draw shootist. He smelled bad.

"Hello, Ben."

"Mr. Robinson," nodding, beckoning toward the jungle, a discreet, soldierly instruction to follow his wraith figure creeping away, now, without delay, noiselessly creeping over the forest floor blanketed in lichen and deadfall and unidentifiable black shapes that mushed underfoot like things wetly alive. Forward we advanced into the dark heart of the recreational grounds, skirting open areas and the relatively unobstructed pathways beneath the pine stands, blazing a trail instead through untamed tracts. The going was harsh. At one point I made out, on my right, the shadowy unlit facade of the boathouse. We stayed clear of it. According to Ben, Turtle Pond was regularly patrolled by hostile Bensons pedaling recreation-services fiberglass paddleboats. This news saddened me. Meredith and I had spent many pleasant hours lazily steering pink or blue or green paddleboats across the pond's tranquil waters. Sometimes, far out at pond's center, beyond sight of either sandy beach or boathouse dock, we'd stop and drop anchor, and Meredith would remove the top of her bathing suit, lie low on her back in the bow of the boat, and sun her beautiful breasts. Oh, love.

"Pay attention, Mr. Robinson."

We were surrounded by picnic tables and waist-high brick-and-mortar grilling stations.

Ben sniffed the air. "Someone's been cooking here."

I smelled nothing. The young Webster led a scavenger hunt of the picnic area. From grill to table to grill we crept. And found, finally, deep within one of the sooty, forlorn pits, fragments of smoldering coal, the scattered remains of embers glowing orange beneath white ash, emitting faint smoky traces. Ben bent down over the grill and nosed at its carbon-encrusted iron crossbars, picked here and there with dirty fingers. He came up with some food, which he put in his mouth.

"Chicken," he said, going down for more.

I rested at one of the tables. These park expeditions were so exhausting. Partly this was due to the tension that came naturally from trekking mapless through a woodland minefield—in my opinion, one absolutely cannot overestimate the effects of something like this, in terms of emotional stress. And there's the purely physical fatigue accompanying so much *careful walking,* which for me involved a lot of involuntary tensing of the calf during step placement (tensing, actually, of the entire foot, leg, hip, back, shoulder, neck, and head areas—in other words, I guess, everywhere, though the calf muscles, and the Achilles tendons in particular, did seem to be the hot suns of that radiant, full-body cramping, aching, throbbing), and, as well, a lot of exaggeratedly high stepping, which burned boatloads of calories in an also involuntary effort to accomplish movement (of whatever kind, in whatever direction) safely above the terrifying surface of the moonlit earth.

Ben was now licking the surface of the grill. Wet sounds and the poor kid's head bobbing over the charred metal. It was hard to watch.

"Ben?"

"Yeah?"

"Are you okay?"

"Sure, fine, great," he said between licks. I took this as pretty clear indication of the alienating effects of malnutrition and exposure to the elements. Obviously Ben was delusional. Still, I had to hand it to him, he was making do, he wasn't complaining, he was a survivor. He stood upright and wiped his mouth with the greasy back of his hand, adjusted his clothes and said, "There's something up ahead I want to show you, Mr. Robinson."

"Lead the way," I told him, though it was getting late and I very much wanted to go home. I was feeling peckish myself. It was well past the dinner hour. I wanted to get home and let Meredith fix me a nice hot meal. A plate of those fish sticks, maybe, from the bottom of the freezer.

Instead of going home for dinner—the sensible thing to do, what with school scheduled to commence in less than twelve hours, and had I even *begun* to prepare for classes?—instead of heading on home while the night was still young, I followed Ben out of the deserted picnic grounds, up a barren hillside crowned with a ghostly playground full of weed-choked, run-down jungle gyms, swing sets, seesaws, and slides;

then past the playground, down the other side of the hill, and onto the rocky path leading to the Japanese garden, at one time one of the finer attractions of Turtle Pond Park. Yes, the Japanese garden was quite the showplace. With its pebble walkways the color of sand, its trickling, carp-ridden brook running between carefully placed, semiprivate "freeform sculpture" seating areas, its exotic imported shrubs waving waxy leaves and tiny pastel blooms that perfumed the air, the Japanese garden made an ideal setting for leisure meditation or a sunny afternoon siesta. And of course it had been, at one time, a favorite meeting place for lovers.

Ben pushed open the garden's rickety bamboo gates. He made a courteous "after you" hand gesture. He said, "This is the place where my father died."

He walked into the garden. Gravel crunched under his feet. A few yards beyond the gateway was a bench, one of those elegant, narrow stone benches, and beside the bench a tree that appeared to be a diminutive variety of cherry. All the trees in this garden had botanical markers driven into the ground beside them, featuring common and taxonomic names, indigenous regions, roles in agronomy, medicinal uses, and so forth. This one wore short branches with delicate, lacy leaves. Ben stood beneath the leaves. He was turned away from me. Shadows and moonlight dappled him. He whispered, "It was night. It was after a rain. Dad was lying on this bench. His clothes were wet. I said, Dad. He didn't answer."

He stared down at the bench. He was remembering, envisioning his father's body. I, too, considered that empty bench, its fine gray contours, those graceful rhomboid legs. The seat looked soft, like a cot. It seemed like a comfortable place to rest. Its polished surface captured night's silver incandescence; the whole bench seemed to glow.

Ben's voice cracked. "Dad's eyes were closed, but he wasn't sleeping."

He was sobbing. Soft muffled whimpers rising from a deep place. I told him, "It's okay, man." Little by little his crying grew louder. Then we were both crying, and the world beyond the borders of the park seemed far away. I said, "Ben, I'm so sorry." And realized, saying it, that I did in fact feel, in a vague, hard-to-pinpoint way, responsible. But for what? Ben's father's death? That was absurd. Or was it? Perhaps I had been wrong, the week previous, perhaps I had been wrong to bury Jim Kunkel's foot. What good was a foot? Stronger medicine was needed to cleanse this tainted grove. The heart! If only I'd buried the heart.

"It's my fault, Mr. Robinson. I let Dad out of my sight. We promised to look after each other. We promised. We *promised.*" He was wailing, a bottomless wailing the likes of which is seldom heard. It was thrilling to be in the company of that sound. I raised the tail of my shirt and blew my nose as Ben wept, "While there's a Benson left alive I won't leave this park. That was my vow to Dad."

He rested his hand on his gun. His fingers caressed the butt of the holstered weapon.

"Violence won't solve anything, Ben."

"Bullshit, Mr. Robinson."

I didn't bother to argue. How could I? In classroom lectures on the medieval Inquisition I'd made the point over and over again that we are all, each and every one of us, heirs to a legacy of blood and grief. Ben's commitment to kill his father's killers was nothing less than testament to this inheritance. Ben Webster had once been one of my favorite pupils. Now he stood before me, lean and stripped down to fighting weight.

"Ben, my home school is scheduled to start tomorrow morning. How would you feel about guest-teaching an elective course in wilderness survival?"

"Me?"

"Think about it. I'm sure it would mean a lot to the kids. You could even lead a field trip here in the park, if you wanted."

His sobbing was diminishing now, becoming gradually quieter. Apparently the teaching gig intrigued him. I said to him, and truly meant this, "Ben, take it from me, you'll be a natural."

Then, to make him feel better, I told him, "You know, Ben, certain ancient cultures believed that the souls of the dead rise up and inhabit a tree. The Christian myth of the resurrection is a sophisticated monotheistic variation on this. Now take this cherry tree here by the bench. Some people—and who is to doubt another's faith, right?—some people would say that maybe, just maybe, your father is *in* that tree."

"In the tree?"

"Yes, in the tree." I went over and placed my hand on a level, shoulder-high bough. I patted the bough and smiled good-naturedly, "Chuck, if you're in there, I just want you to know that an awful lot of people care an awful lot about you, especially your son."

Ben looked at me with a glassy expression. He told me he wasn't sure how he felt about any of this, about his father being in the tree; it sounded strange to him. Besides which, he went on to explain, his dad was buried a good distance away from the cherry tree. Ben pointed, "Over there. By the brook."

"Is there a tree over there? Strictly speaking, it needn't be a tree. Your dad could be in a bush or the flowers or even a blade of grass. Or if he's near the brook he might be in one of those goldfish."

"There aren't any goldfish. I ate them."

"Then I guess he's in *you,* isn't he?"

The boy wore a stricken look. I backpedaled, saying, "Heh heh, just kidding. Don't take things so seriously. It was only an idea. Anyway, it's getting late and I've got a long walk ahead of me."

"Mr. Robinson?"

"Yeah, Ben?"

"Do you believe that stuff about trees and flowers and fish and all?"

Good question. I explained to Ben that, in this instance, my beliefs were of secondary importance, except as a compliment or contrast to his, whatever they might be, vis-à-vis the whole "spirit afterlife" issue. I also pointed out to Ben that, whatever his personal convictions in the matter, it so happens that many societies, around the globe and throughout history, have regarded enclosed gardens like this one, the one we were standing in, as sacrosanct. "Your father's around here somewhere, Ben. You can bet on it."

With that I took my leave. Halfway up the hill to the abandoned playground, I turned and looked back. The moon was high. I could see, by its silvery light, the entire Japanese garden: the brook, the walkways, the decorative pagoda; and, not far from the garden's bamboo gates, hard by the glowing bench, the figure of Ben, hugging the cherry tree, weeping. I decided, then and there, that I'd come back here soon and bury, as a symbol of the lifeblood that passes from fathers to their sons, the ex-mayor's freezer-paper-wrapped heart. Not, though, without first thawing it out and letting the kids in school pass it around. Jim's vital organs would make splendid show-and-tell exhibits. Maybe not the genitals. The genitals would serve better in a high school setting. But Jim's liver, lung, spleen, hand, and assorted viscera—that stuff would be super at any age. I got so revved up, planning the classes I could build around Jim's anatomy, that I completely forgot the dangers of walking through Turtle Pond Park. I was relaxed and happy, excited about the future, eager to get home and tell Meredith all about my encounter with Ben, how I'd been able to make him feel a little better about his loss. Also, I wanted to make love without contraception, because spending time with Ben had made me imagine how great it would be to have a son of my own, a son who would kill for me, and whom I'd name Ben. And while jogging past the boathouse and into the dense woods, I pictured all the things we'd do together, my son Ben and I, the ball games we'd play and the bikes we'd ride and the fish we'd catch. These father/son tableaux images looked beautiful to me. So beautiful, in fact, that it began to seem inconceivable that Meredith would be anything but wildly enthusiastic about the idea of a son. Certainly she'd share my desire to have sex without contraception, wherever we happened to be at the moment: on the kitchen floor, or on a table or the counter by the sink basin, or on the fold-out sleeper sofa in the living room; or how about out back in the wet sandy mud by the trench! Or just plain in bed, beneath soft cotton sheets, nice and easy, in order to conceive right away.

The forest floor was dark. Not much moonlight reached beneath the tangled canopy of leaves overhead. Ground-level creeping vines were everywhere, there was no avoiding them, it was a real obstacle course. The image of Meredith was my beacon. I kept thinking about how lovely she'd be, pregnant. It was invigorating, sexy in an elemental and potent way, stampeding through the thorns with a hard-on, beating a path to her. By the time I got to the car I was pretty torn up, and I felt good about it. Each scar, each bruise, each bleeding wound, was a badge signifying passion, intensity, and the untamable fires of procreative love.

I jumped in the Toyota. The streets were empty. I navigated in cool style, shifting down before banking on the right-angle curves, four-wheel drifting into the opposing lane with that satisfying high-RPM, low-gear engine whine, then easing out the clutch and accelerating onto the straightaway, surfing the whole road and going fast. I'm not, as a rule, in favor of reckless driving, speed for the sake of speed. However, it's a good thing, from time to time, to let go of worldly cares and flatten the accelerator to the floor. Tonight the Toyota performed admirably—for a mid-price. On Main Street I caught a glimpse of the BIG WEEKEND CLEARANCE SALE! ALL MENSWEAR HALF PRICE! EVERYTHING MUST GO! sign in Dick Morton's clothing store window, the same sign I'd noticed earlier in the day, on the way to the park; and I remembered my plan to pick up a new bow tie for school. Now, unfortunately, it was too late. The store was long closed. For an instant, cruising along at close to eighty miles per hour, I had an amusing vision of myself slamming on the brakes and skidding to a halt, leaping from the driver's seat, hurling *Martyrs Mirror* through the plate glass fronting Morton's store, and ducking in and looting a bow tie—just one tie, that's all, in a muted paisley or classic two-tone rep stripe, or better yet a bold, high-fashion silk, something tasteful yet with flair to suit my mood. I wouldn't even care if I got cut on a shard of window glass. Big deal, what's another cut?

At home, the lights were on. I wheeled into the driveway and secured the hand brake. There was blood on the steering wheel, blood staining the gearshift. A warm trickle made its way down my neck. It felt sweet. I gathered the books and went around back and up the wood-plank steps to the kitchen door.

I could hear, from within the house, the deep and rhythmic pounding of drums.

"Meredith, it's me, I'm home," kicking open the door, marching inside. The drum tape was booming loudly enough for the neighbors to hear. The last thing we needed was a noise dispute with the Kinseys or the McElroys. Those kinds of confrontations invariably create discomfort.

But not such discomfort, I'm afraid, as that caused me by the sight of Meredith sprawled on her back on the living room floor, on the plush blue carpet, her nightgown twisted up around her waist, her arms and legs thrashing and kicking and drenched in perspiration that glistened amber beneath the living room's low-wattage lamplight.

"Hey, Meredith."

She jerked from side to side. Her hair was a mess. Fish

bones and seashells lay in piles on the coffee table; more shells were scattered across the floor. There were so many shells. The rug was transformed—it was like a scaled-down seabed environment, a clutter of cowries and oysters and cockles and scallops that glowed liquid pink on the inside; and zebra-striped star shells, spiny-edged and no bigger than coat buttons; and top-shaped shells like iridescent children's toys, their nautiloid exteriors gaudy with spots, speckles, and blotches.

Meredith opened her mouth. Her tongue stuck out. It wasn't sexy, it was grotesque, and it upset me to watch it. I cleared a space and put the books on the coffee table, knelt beside her and said, "Honey?"

She was shivering and her face was white. I cradled her head in my lap. Her breasts beneath her lavender nightgown rose and fell with her breathing; her head was heavy. Fine strands of black hair clung to her forehead. I brushed the hair from her face. And I tried to avoid smearing blood on her, blood from my hands, but a little got on her cheek. I wet my shirttail with spit and wiped it away. Here in the warmly lit living room I could examine the full damage of scratching on my arms. They looked, my arms, as if they'd been assailed by frenzied kittens.

Meredith coughed a liquid cough. Her hands waved and her body trembled; her eyes opened, closed, opened. In a soft, faraway voice, she asked, "Who's there?"

"It's me. Pete."

"Pete?"

"Your husband."

"Husband?"

What was there to say to this? I stroked Meredith's head,

massaged the skin around the temples. My honey's arms arced upward, then down, dog-paddling air in fluid, openhanded sweeps, dancing in rhythm with the drums and her own decelerated heartbeat. She stretched her legs, did a few lateral frog kicks, wiggled a bit, and sighed seductively, "Come on in, the water's great."

Was she kidding? What was she thinking? Had she forgotten what happened the last time I'd "come on in"? Did she want me to die?

Meredith was not, I realized at this point, as I watched her twist and roll on the carpet—she was not, strictly speaking, human.

As if to bear this out she made one of those fish faces of hers. This would be cute if it weren't so frightening in its implications. She puckered her lips, scrunched her nose, shook her head in tiny, back-and-forth darting motions. What was she doing? Feeding? She seemed so far away. Her hand caressed my neck. Languid fingers tickling, the flick of a nail; it was pleasing and sad at the same time. I took her hand in mine, guided it searching up over my unshaved, dirty face. I kissed her palm, then opened my mouth and inserted a finger (her middle, the longest), sucking it down all the way to the knuckle. "Oh, Meredith," I moaned—gurgled, actually; Meredith's finger went quite far into my mouth, reached gag depth, almost; I could feel the nail poking and tickling the back of my throat, making my eyes water—"Oh, Mewedith, don' you know I lub you?"

But she was too submerged to hear; she was out of earshot, swimming away to wherever.

"*Come back,*" I wanted to call to her.

After a while the drum tape ran its course. The hollow beating faded and ended, and the tape deck clicked off. The room became silent except for outside night sounds: a distant, shrieking seabird; gusting wind that blew a tree branch irregularly and repeatedly scraping against the back wall of the house; and, inside, the low vibrating rumble of the refrigerator motor shuddering on in the kitchen; and the sounds of our breathing, my wife's and mine. Meredith's breaths were the bottomless unlabored exhalations of a peaceful sleeper. My own were raspy, wheezy—I was getting some phlegm. Maybe I was coming down with a bug. What a rotten way to kick off the new school year. It's important, during the first days of getting to know the students, and letting them get to know you, to be in top physical and mental form. Children tend to be acutely sensitive to any hint, in an authority figure, of weakness or despair; they'll take advantage of it, they'll be all over you. I don't like to come off as a disciplinarian, but experience has shown that an atmosphere of order and control, established right off the bat, will prevail throughout the year, while laxity, permissiveness, any implied promise of unrealistic classroom "freedoms"—these things can be hell to correct, and can, unchecked, lead to anarchy. For this reason I typically adopt a "stern taskmaster" persona, informing the little scofflaws that they'll have to stow away their favorite toys, the ones they've brought for the first day, they can forget about "playtime" for now; then giving a series of demanding in-class reading assignments, followed by a multiple-choice pop quiz on some arcane topic in history and, to top things off, hours of homework that gets graded harshly.

Meredith opened her eyes. She stretched and yawned. Her

brown body smelled oceany. I wanted to fuck her. I wanted to begin making our baby. Would this ever happen?

We huddled like slumber-partying children alone in the house, free to stay up late for the *Creature Feature* late show on TV, slightly uncomfortable on overstuffed cushions hauled from the sofa and dispersed like mattresses across the rug. Meredith pushed aside her scattered shell collection and turned to lie on her side. She was looking directly at me, giving me a *look,* as if she were waiting for me to explain my whole life. But it was my wife doing the explaining: "Everybody's down on the reef, Pete. All our friends. Jerry and Rita and Abe and Bill and Barbara and Tom and everybody. And hey, guess what? It's true about Abe and Rita. They are in love. You see, they're both manatee, and Jerry's a tuna."

"A tuna?"

"Yeah. Can you believe that? And guess what Bill is."

"I don't know."

"Guess."

"Seriously, I don't know."

"*Guess,* Pete."

"Um. A clam."

"Right!" She picked up a clamshell from the floor beside her and, gesturing with it, said, "Bill's a bivalve. He doesn't know this of course. He's too busy drinking to have any real insights into himself. But I've seen him on the reef, buried in the sand in one of these."

"How about that," I said. Then inquired, coolly, whether everyone in town was some kind of sea creature, or if there were, maybe, other ruminants, grazers, or for that matter any manner of vertebrate land mammals to be found locally.

Meredith told me that, as far as she knew, pretty much everyone we socialized with—those were her words: "pretty much everyone we socialize with"—was a continental shelf–dweller, but that I shouldn't worry about it, certainly *some* of my kind were roaming around *somewhere.*

How upsetting. I don't profess to know much about the massacre of the Plains buffalo; it's not my period of study. Nevertheless it was all I could do, thinking about it, to keep from becoming paralyzed with despondency. What could I possibly say? What could I do? It was the middle of the night and I felt alone. I said to my wife, "School tomorrow, hon. Why don't you go on up to bed. I want to do a few last-minute things around the house," then roused myself and made a groggy, stumbling tour of the downstairs, locking doors and turning off lights, shutting off the main power on the stereo, checking, out of habit, that the gas burners on the stove were, indeed, off. The stuffed bison, property of the Juvenile department of the public library, was still lying on its furry brown back, in the kitchen corner, behind a chair, where I'd tossed it the week before. I drank some tap water and went downstairs to the basement to look it over as a homeroom location. Yes, the basement was the place. With its fluorescent-lit, windowless walls, its low, cracked ceiling and unpainted concrete floor featuring sunk-in rusted iron drain gratings, the basement had a certain institutional feel, unlike the rest of the house, which was distractingly domestic in appearance and mood, as well as being full of breakables. Set up seats, tack up a bulletin board, and the basement would easily resemble any number of classrooms in real schools. There was a musty wet odor everywhere, and a fair number of spiders seemed to've made homes among the water pipes running beneath the kitchen and the downstairs bathroom, but these drawbacks were minor. The smell of mildew would soon be masked by the milky-scented breath of toddlers. The spiders could figure in a science project. I made a mental note to this effect—webs: compare and contrast—before trudging upstairs and padding from room to room, selecting furnishings from various places in the house, to lend the basement a friendly, welcoming air. From the living room I filched nature magazines, the ceramic bowl holding dried rose petals, several gaily embroidered throw pillows (for an informal "nap nook" beneath the insulated black pipes rising and twisting like swollen arteries from the top of the antiquated furnace), a straight-backed chair, and—not to forget—those textbooks rescued from the park. Maybe, with Meredith on religion and me on history, and using *Martyrs Mirror* as a source, we might team-teach a seminar on Pain and Sacrifice. ("This class ponders the ways that suffering has, historically, abetted the development of 'personal' consciousness and the autonomous Self, from Saint Augustine to the Moderns.") I also threw in a few "leisure reading" volumes of my own, picture books offering photographic tours of foreign lands, great houses, and award-winning gardens. From the hallway I got a coatrack. Hanging on a wall were a set of sentimental watercolors of boats; these I tacked up in the basement stairwell. A pretty bathroom throw rug made the unpainted floor seem less cold. Lamps warmed the unclean white walls. I arranged, in columnar order, as benches, several storage trunks, battered steamers trimmed in bug-eaten leather and latched with brass clasps hammered to resemble fantastic animal claws. One of the trunks was extremely heavy because it contained a collection of tattered, yellowing school papers from the past: lesson plans, copies of student papers too praiseworthy to discard, end-of-year personnel performance reports. It was impossible to resist a moment's reading. One report began, "While Mr. Robinson is decidedly one of our more charismatic and engaging lecturers, and while students appear to be positively influenced by Mr. Robinson's enthusiasm for the material, it might be wished that Mr. Robinson's podium style were, in future, less rhapsodic." Another proclaimed: "Mr. Robinson's novel ideas concerning history and the formation of social systems make fascinating food for thought. However, the committee wonders whether show-and-tell lessons which teach the interogation [*sic*] techniques of the Middle Ages constitute suitable educational fare for third-graders." Blah, blah, blah. What a relief, to get free, once and for all, of administrative interference. Wasn't this the whole idea behind the home school? Freedom? Freedom to reach out and touch the hearts and minds of the coming new generation—and no bureaucrats around to get in the way. With a concussive bang that sent dust clouds rolling through the somber basement air, I dropped the lid on the big crate of school files, upended it, and plunked it front and center at the head of the class: here was a fine podium. Every school must have its mascot. I retrieved the stuffed bison from the kitchen floor and awarded it pride of place, smack in the middle of everything, on top of the rusted iron drain grating sunk like an escape hatch in the poured foundation of the house. On my way back upstairs I paused a moment. The 1:32-scale dungeon model rested on its worktable. It had gathered, over the preceding weeks, a white patina of dust. I picked up a sheet of sandpaper and a chunk of balsa roughly whittled in the form of a "tree trunk" beheading dais. The dungeon walls begged for detailing: there were cracks to be carved; spiderwebs in my own basement suggested possibilities for rubber cement webs draped over the prison's scaled-down hay bed, which I'd decided to pattern on the one in *Martyrs Mirror,* the one in the engraved plate depicting "Georg Wanger in the Dungeon." There remained the question of the model's narrative content. For instance, those reptiles. Actually whittling a snake—hissing, contorted and looming to strike out and murder an infidel—seemed beyond my journeyman-artisan capabilities. Frogs were feasible. But frogs weren't especially threatening. How about an alligator? Implanting a nontraditional signifier (soft-sculpture subtropical crocodilian), within a traditional environment (musty European penal cell), could serve to recontextualize the scene, thereby transcending generic medieval-prison-image associations, upsetting viewer expectations, and creating a startling new "here and now" dungeon reality. Yes. I continued up the staircase, passed through the quiet, breezy kitchen—stopping along the way for another drink of tap water—then went out back to inspect the yard as a playground. The dark of night had passed, and the ocean air felt wet and warm. Dawn's first rays of sun threw ashen light over tall palms and the roofs of neighboring houses. Meredith's spear tips cast shadows into the depths of the pit. It was that sweaty time of morning when the first songbirds begin chirping. I had a bad case of fuzzy dry-mouth and one of those sickening behind-the-eyes headaches. And the scratches on my body had begun to ache in the throbbing way that presages infection. Before long, excitable kids would arrive in armor-plated station wagons driven by sexy moms. For now, though, the sandy, wet backyard grass felt cool to lie on. I loosened my belt, tugged up my socks, leaned back, closed my eyes, and did a creative-visualization relaxation exercise in which I breathed deeply and imagined myself roaming wild and free across the western Great Plains. Tall prairie grasses bent beneath wind and the stamping hooves of a vast, snorting herd. My herd! Slowly we made our way across open land. It was a bright new day. The sun was a silver wafer. Piles of our dung sent up steam. Tick-eating birds swooped down to perch on our matted backs. Here everything had its own rich smell. Clover, mint, fresh wild hay. Overhead, hawks lofted on convective drafts rising from the warm valleys where, in our multitudes, we gathered: a majestic, grass-chewing nation.

I lowered my fuzzy head to the rich green earth, and gathered in my mouth a big sweet clump of its wonderful, grassy food.

The next thing I knew, I was being kicked in the ribs by small shoes. A child's voice was saying, "Okay, mister, nice and easy now."

"Keep him covered. If he tries anything funny, let him have it in the foot," another child's voice said.

A pair of freckle-faced boys stood over me. The boys appeared to be about ten years old. They were identical in every respect. Each was armed with a venal-looking longbow strung with razor-sharp hunting ordnance.

It was the Harris twins, Matt and Larry, with their bow-and-arrow sets.

In as cautious a voice as I could summon, I spoke to them. "Easy, guys."

The sun floated high in the sky. It must've been well past the time for school to begin. I was dirty and my clothes were badly grass-stained. I said to the boys, "Put down your weapons. I'm your teacher."

"If you're our teacher, how come you're out here eating the grass?" asked the first boy.

"I wasn't."

"You were. Like an animal. We watched," the brother said, obnoxiously.

I told them, "When you get to be my age, and you have the fear of death, you'll understand these things. Did you remember to pack your bag lunches?"

"Our mom's got them," they exclaimed in unison. Motioning with their bows and arrows, they directed me to rise. "Put your hands on your head and walk toward the house," one of them commanded.

Did they think this was a game? Once school got under way I'd teach them a thing or two about endangering innocent people's lives.

On the other hand, you had to hand it to them—and their parents. Carl and Deborah Harris had obviously done marvelous work in training their young sons for sentry duty. These boys were alert, cautious, under control; they weren't taking any chances. Even now, as we came around the side yard and passed through the tall hedge of blooming jasmine bordering the walkway to the front porch, they kept a safe distance behind me. One of them called ahead, "Hey, Mom."

Deborah Harris was standing on the porch. She clutched, in her middle-aged hands, those aforementioned bag lunches. Several other mothers and their anxious, dressed-up kids gathered in klatches on the grass and at the foot of the porch steps, like people at a church function. I recognized several youngsters from Story Time at the library. There was Steven Moody, the sensitive boy, with his overprotective mom, Sheila. And there was the boy named David, holding his red-headed infant brother, Tim. The despondent-looking girl, the one who always appeared to be weeping—what was her name? Jane?—perched on the bottommost porch step. She was drawing, in the dirt, with a stick, pictures of what appeared to be fish.

In all, there were ten kids. Enough for a start. The future beckoned. The children clutched lunches and toy animals, their dolls and plastic guns.

In the middle of the yard, near a clump of purple wildflowers, was the little auburn-haired sweetie, the sexy child with the lace-up oxfords decorated with friendly smiling schnauzers' faces.

"Hey there, Sarah," I called to her.

"It's the monster!" Sarah shrieked. Her mother reached down and grabbed her hand, wrenching Sarah forcefully from my path. From behind my back a Harris twin, in a voice like a soldier's, though higher-pitched, ordered, "Stop right there. Don't move your hands from your head. Tell my mother who you are."

I could feel the points of arrows tickling me in the kidney region. What a situation. Here I was, briar-scratched, unwashed and unshaved, wearing bloody clothes and one of those "dirt" tans, my fingernails black with grime and my hair standing straight up off my head, the way it always does in the morning, like a set of those bony jutting dorsal plates purported to have graced the backs of certain dinosaurs.

"Hello, Deborah. It's me, Pete."

"Oh my God."

Fortunately, Sarah's mother, Mrs. Miller, who'd been present at the library for Saturday morning Story Time, when I'd brought in the destroyed *Egyptian Book of the Dead,* stepped forward and said, somewhat sarcastically, "More lawn work, I suppose, Mr. Robinson?"

"Right you are. Getting the playing field together. So much to do. So little time."

"Isn't that the truth," said Deborah Harris, relaxing a little. Though only a little. She inquired, "What sort of athletic program do you have in mind, Mr. Robinson?"

Before I could think of an answer, one of her sons thrust an arrow hard at my back. "We found him eating grass."

"Heh heh. Kids," I said.

As luck would have it, Deborah Harris was one of those parents who always believe another adult before their own children. She glared at her sons. "Put away those bows right now and behave yourselves."

"But Mom!"

The thing to do was get shed of all these mothers, then hustle the youngsters down to the basement. The sooner class began, the sooner the PETE ROBINSON IS THE ONLY CONCEIVABLE CHOICE FOR MAYOR campaign could start rolling.

Deborah, who seemed to've assumed a spokeswoman role for the assembly of parents, said, "Are you sure you're feeling well, Mr. Robinson?"

"What do you mean?"

"You look a little tired is all."

Talk about understatements. Thank God for Jenny Jordan, turning up the drive in her beat-up Volvo. Susy and Brad hopped up and down wildly on the back seat. Jenny tooted the horn and waved, and we all waved back. It was as if her arrival signaled that the world was normal and good. The day could proceed.

"Hi, Brad! Hi, Susy!" I called.

"Hello, Mr. Robinson," yelled my star pupils, leaping from the Volvo and skipping up the walkway to the house. Brad carried his Erector Set missile launcher, enormous and looking dangerously real in his small, fat arms. Susy gripped, by the hair, her disheveled doll.

"Sorry we're late," Jenny said, coming across the grass in sundress and sandals.

"No problem. We're spending a few minutes getting to know one another. Jenny, have you met Deborah Harris? Deborah, this is Jenny Jordan, and this is Susy and this is Brad. Susy, Brad, say hello to your new classmates, Matt and Larry." And so on. Hellos all around:

"Hi. I'm Sheila Moody, and this is Steven. What do you say when you meet someone, Steven?"

"Hello."

"Steven will be a second-grader this year. Isn't that right, sweetie?"

And:

"This is David, and this is his brother Tim. Tim's gotten to be a very good walker recently. You don't think he's too young for school, do you?"

And:

"Let me get this straight. You're Matt. And you're Larry. Oh, you're Larry?"

And:

"Our Jane always gets frightened when she has to leave the house. Eventually she calms down. Don't pay her any mind if she cries."

And:

"I see. Larry's the one with the bump on the back of the head. How'd you get that bump, Larry?"

And:

"Well, Susy would be grade two, I guess. Brad's still preschool."

And:

"I think it's so fascinating that your daughter's name is Hope."

After an interval I called out, "Everybody! Folks! Can I have your attention?"

The yard fell quiet. Moms and kids stared my way. "I'm not much for speeches, but I think it's appropriate at this time to say a few words in connection with this proud moment in education—"

That's as far as I got. The front door of the house opened, and Meredith walked out onto the porch. She was wearing a low-cut purple dress. Her hair was pulled back in a ponytail. Strung around her neck were tiny, spectacular seashells. She looked like royalty. As if on cue my audience turned, resting wide, admiring gazes on her. She opened her arms and said, "Come in, everyone. There's juice and coffee in the kitchen."

I took up the rear, waited while the line of parents and children progressed into the house. Meredith was charming and gracious, offering and receiving pecks on the cheek and polite social hugs from the women, patting the children on the head and saying things like "What a pretty doll," and "My, that's quite a gun you've got."

When it came my turn to go inside, she said, "Excuse me, Pete, where are the other teachers?"

"Oh."

In fact, I'd failed to contact any of them. What can be said about this?

"I forgot."

"You forgot?"

Lamely I blurted, "To call them."

"I don't *believe* this." Her fury was exquisite. She was livid, actually scowling. "You might at least have washed your face and brushed your teeth. They're green." She turned, seashell necklace clattering, and marched inside to make like a hostess with the refreshments. I slunk in after her and chugged some coffee myself, taking care to wash it around like a rinse. Kids were exploring the downstairs, and moms were expressing gratitude for our selfless dedication, etc., etc. No one missed me when I took a moment to rush upstairs and tie on a bright red "first day" bow tie (a previous year's); it took a while to get the knot right—I like a tight, precisely defined knot, with a certain soft, wrinkly flare in the wings of the tie. I don't go for a lot of dandyish, straight-out wing extension. I had to do several retyings, because my hands were trembling and my fingers were sore from cuts. I believe it's important to look as together as possible for the start of the year; it's a small gesture, though not trivial; it engenders respect and makes me feel ready to do my job. I think of it—putting on the tie, adjusting it just so—as analogous to an actor's preparations for the stage, an athlete's warm-up before the game.

On my way downstairs I stopped off in the bedroom and purloined our digital alarm clock/radio. What's a school without a bell? And in the front hallway I exchanged perfunctory farewells with the parents. I'd wanted to get a moment alone with Jenny, if only to admire her beautiful, sandaled feet, but she was already gone, driving away. Little Jane, weeping as usual, had to be coaxed from her mother's skirts. The girl called Hope was hiding beneath the kitchen table. I called out instructions. "Okay kids, fall in. Make a single-file line and follow me. No pushing or shoving on the stairs."

Down we went. The basement was cool and damp. It felt like a subterranean bunker hideaway. Matt and Larry, piling down the steps and noticing the dungeon model on its table, exclaimed, "Wow. Cool." I went in search of a wall socket. There was one behind the furnace. I set the alarm for the time on the display and plugged it in, and it erupted like a siren in the hollow concrete room, scaring Jane into fresh tears. The infant Tim, who was being carried down the steps by his older brother, also let out a howl. I said, "This is the bell. When you hear it you will assume your seats and take out paper and pencil."

"Can we sit anywhere?" asked Susy Jordan, racing to claim a place at the head of the class. She hurled herself onto a trunk and announced, "This is my seat."

"Fine. You sit there. Brad, go sit next to your sister."

"Do I have to?"

"*Brad,*" said Susy. Brad skulked over and settled onto the edge of the trunk. His sister pinched his arm, scolded him in low tones, "Don't make trouble, brat."

"Don't call me brat."

"Don't be one."

"Hey, hey," I said. Susy beamed. "I apologize for my brother, Mr. Robinson." It cheered me to know that at least one potential discipline problem would be taken in hand without intervention on my part. The other problems, it seemed clear, would be Matt and Larry Harris, who remained over by the dungeon, picking up pieces of the model, holding them aloft in the bare-bulb light, saying things like "This is nothing. I could build this shit."

"Guys, put that stuff down and come over here behind Susy and Brad." I didn't want these two in the back of the class—the traditional place for class clowns, spitball throwers, and general fuckups.

"What do we do with these?" asked one, displaying his powerful longbow. "Under the stairs," I told them. "That goes for everybody. All toys in the cardboard box beneath the stairs. Pronto."

One by one, the kids came forward and consigned their playthings to the box. Jane's toy, it turned out, was the stick she'd been using, earlier, to draw dirt pictures of fish. This sad fact earned from Sarah, of the wet red mouth and dog-faced shoes, the harsh comment "That's your toy? A *stick*?"

More sobbing from Jane. I had to step in and say, "One of the things I hope to teach you this semester is the importance of tolerating diversity. Who can tell me what the word 'diversity' means? No one? Diversity means difference. We're all different people, with different beliefs, different styles of clothes, different toys and hobbies. And what are some of our special hobbies? Anyone?"

"Helping my mom in the kitchen."

"Superb hobby, Susy. Uh, let's see. Steven. Steven, do you have a favorite hobby that you like a lot?"

"Snorkeling in the pool."

"Another fine hobby. David, how about you? What do you do for pleasure and amusement?"

David, still cradling Tim in his arms, said, from the back of the class, "My mom and dad hardly ever come home, so I have to spend most of my time taking care of my brother. Does that count?"

"Well, actually, no."

From overhead I could hear Meredith's footsteps, the creaking of the floorboards. Meredith was probably cleaning juice glasses and coffee cups in the kitchen. Or setting out napkins and plates for lunch break. After a moment she came partway down the basement stairs—interrupting the Harris twins' Byzantine tales of neighborhood bow-hunting expeditions under cover of night—and said, "Excuse me a moment. Pete, the drain's clogged again."

"Be right up, hon." I went to the metal tool cabinet and got out the plumber's snake. I coiled the snake like a whip and instructed, "No one leaves his or her seat. There will be *no* talking. If I hear a single sound from down here, you will *all* be held accountable."

Upstairs, Hope was still hunkered down under the table.

Chair legs caged her. I hadn't even noticed her absence from the class. Meredith said, "She won't come out. Poor baby."

I pulled back a chair and crouched down, got eye level. "Hope, don't you like school?"

"No."

"All your friends are here. We're going to have a swell time. I have a lot of fun games planned for later. Won't you come downstairs?"

"Leave her be, Pete. I'll stay up here with her. She'll be okay. Look at this drain."

Sure enough, it was backed up to the rim; piled cups and glasses loomed like a crystal city submerged beneath soapy water that stung my wounds when I reached in for the food trap. I cleared space around the drain and slithered the flexible copper snake into the pipe. It went a foot. I could not force it farther.

"Fuck."

"Not in front of children, Pete."

"Right. Sorry."

I administered a couple more futile plunges with the snake. Meredith watched over my shoulder. Whatever was in there, it was really in there.

"Do we have Drāno?" I asked.

"You're not supposed to pour Drāno through standing water, I don't think."

"Hmn. Maybe this'll drain out over time. We can pour Drāno in later."

I re-coiled the wet snake and bent down to peer at Hope beneath the table. She'd gathered herself into a ball, pale child's arms tightly wrapping dirty knees. Her staring eyes were wild.

"Don't make me drag you out of there."

"Pete!"

"Okay, okay. Relax. I was only kidding." And then, to Hope, this warning: "If you get behind in your lessons you'll have take-home makeup assignments."

On the way downstairs I made sure to shut the basement door, locking the bolt securely from the inside, to prevent any more intrusions.

The kids, all nine, were sitting quietly on their trunks. All except Tim, who was still in his brother's lap, rocking, whimpering.

As I came down the creaking steps David raised his hand. "Mr. Robinson?"

"Yes?"

"I need to change him."

"Can it wait?"

"I don't think so, sir."

How very tiresome. "All right, go ahead." David hoisted his brother and headed for the stairs, but I blocked his path. He said, "It's best if I do this in a bathroom."

"I don't mind if you do it here. You can rest Tim on top of the furnace. The rest of us will continue with class, and you can listen in."

David didn't look enthusiastic about changing his little brother on the furnace, but I insisted it was okay, he didn't have to be squeamish, it wouldn't distract the rest of us in the least. Finally he gave in and retired to the back of the basement, where, in dim, forty-watt light, he unsnapped Tim's jumper. I took my place behind the podium. I kept the plumber's snake by my side. Susy and Brad sat at attention in the first row, ready to jot notes. Matt and Larry hunched forward like hoodlums in their seats. Steven and Sarah, sharing the trunk behind the Harrises', made a sweet couple. Next came Jane. Near her feet the bison mascot rested on its sunk-in drain grating. I exclaimed, in my best oratorial style, "Everybody, repeat after me. Diversity! Tolerance!"

"Diversity. Tolerance," said Susy Jordan.

"All of you. Diversity! Tolerance!"

"Diversity. Tolerance."

"That doesn't sound very convincing. Louder now. Diversity! Tolerance!"

"Diversity. Tolerance."

"Much better. Again with feeling. I want to *hear* you. You too, David. Raise the rafters. Together now. Diversity! Tolerance!"

"Diversity! Tolerance!" the youths chorused.

"Excellent. That's your class motto. Learn it and don't forget it."

It was also, I'd decided, a perfect centerpiece slogan for the mayoral campaign. Listening to those kids chant gave me such a high.

"How's it going, David?" I called to the boy performing childcare at the back of the room.

"Almost finished, Mr. Robinson," waving a soiled disposable diaper in the air. Its sweet, rotted-fruit smell filled the room. The Harris twins, having gotten a whiff, held their noses and trembled with church giggles. Getting Matt and Larry to hush was easy—all I had to do was make a reproachful face and subtly caress the copper tail of the plumber's snake dangling like a live thing over the leather edge of the upended trunk/podium. Meanwhile David was searching in vain for a place to dispose of brother Tim's used diaper. Missing from the basement was a garbage can. The one available cardboard box was in use as toy storage. I told David to please fold the diaper neatly and slide it beneath the furnace.

"Mr. Robinson?"

"Yes, Susy?"

"What are those spots on your arms?"

She was right. The cuts and scratches, formerly reddish, light abrasions, had, over the course of the night and the early morning, blossomed into purplish volcanic flowering splotches. Had the thorns responsible for these welts contained some malevolent toxin? The pain, now that I paused to think about it, to consider it, was acute. I grimaced, told Susy not to worry, it was nothing, an allergic reaction perhaps; and she said, "There's a *big* one on your neck." Then suddenly Tim was crying again, unintelligible sputtering howls that charged the basement air with anxious chaos. I shouted at David, "Would you mind keeping him quiet?" David stuffed a pacifier in Tim's face. Sarah, who'd been watching, over her shoulder, the entire changing operation, reprimanded David for his lack of gentleness.

"Mind your own business," he told her.

Sarah turned to me for support. She was an ace flirt for a toddler; she had those enormous eyes, that moist, father-seducing grin. I think it is fair to say that the feelings she aroused in her teacher are best left, in the interests of seemliness, undiscussed. I said to her, "Generally, methods of child rearing are considered to be discretionary. Who can tell us what 'discretionary' means? Anyone? Yes, Susy?"

"Private?"

"Close enough."

Sarah pouted. Under her breath, yet loud enough to be heard, she growled, "*Monster.*"

The whole class tensed. You could feel it. The silence was immaculate, breathless, complete. Even Tim quit his yowling. It broke my heart to have to exercise discipline on a cutie like Sarah. I had no choice. I addressed the class in a sonorous voice, "It is my sad burden to advise you all of the consequences of calumny and slander in the classroom."

They looked nervous. This at least was gratifying. I waited awhile in order to let the kids worry sufficiently (a tried-and-true discipline technique—abject silence), before continuing, "Sarah, please rise and come forward."

She got to her feet. Attempted unsteady progress toward the head of the class. She was, obviously, unnerved. I encouraged her to *please* get herself moving, and I asked her, "What do you think we ought to do with you?"

She gazed floorward. Her shoulders were trembling. Sarah's soft lips moved, but no sound came out.

"Class, what should we do with Sarah?"

It was only a matter of time before a hand went up. Then another. And another.

"Steven?"

"I think Sarah should apologize."

"Thank you, Steven. David?"

"Let her stay late after school and write a hundred times or something?"

"Make her do blackboard-washing duty," offered Jane, though there were no blackboards to wash.

Leave it to Susy. "Expel her."

After that I didn't hazard calling on the Harris twins for their suggestions. There's a limit. I pointed to a musty unlit corner of the basement, where fungus carpeted the floor and web-enshrouded water pipes plunged down through holes in the ceiling. The straight-backed chair, the one from the living room, sat facing a wall.

"Go over there and sit down, young lady. When you've decided you feel ready to behave, maybe you can come back and try to be a member of this class."

Sarah walked to that chair like she thought it was electric. Her auburn-curled head bobbed low; her arms hung at her sides as if drained of life. I couldn't help noticing how the basement's lamplight cast Sarah's shadow onto the dark far wall: as Sarah walked away from the light, so did her shadow—diminishing, rapidly, in height—walk away from us; it was as if a phantom Sarah were speeding away on a long journey. It was heartbreaking. It was too much for Jane, alone at the back of the class, to bear; she broke down sobbing. Tim spit out his pacifier and joined in. The noise became gruesome. I shouted, "Hey! Hey!" as the wailing swelled to higher and higher intensity. Sure enough, the knob of the basement door at the crest of the stairs began rattling, and Meredith's muffled voice tumbled down from on high. "What's all that crying? Pete! Why is this door locked?"

"It's okay, honey. No problem. No need to worry. Everything's under control," I called, merrily.

And, to the kids: "Let's all settle down. All right?"

Then, loudly: "Listen up and I'll tell you about a time before democracy was born. A time when affliction and suffering were the bread and water of daily life. Ignorance and rampaging diseases governed men's lives. Diversity in all its forms was punishable by death or imprisonment, and you were guilty until proven innocent."

Well, the children did listen. They craned forward on their storage trunks. Their eyes opened wide, their weeping diminished; they wore studious faces. Sarah, her face to the wall, even little Sarah seemed to tune in—you could see it in her hypererect posture. Of course, that might've been the chair. For my part, I was in the groove, gathering steam and rolling through the terrible centuries, telling tale after tale to the finest audience in the world.

"And then what happened?" the kids would eagerly demand whenever I paused for breath.

"He received the tongue screws and never was able to utter a word again, but using blood as ink, he wrote a diary of his dying days in a worm-plagued prison cell, and was declared a martyr," I would tell them.

Or:

"They took hold of her and viciously tore the flesh from her sides, only to discover that her smile grew, and she was in ecstasies for her pain."

Or:

"Flames leapt into air, licking the tender soles of their feet, and yet they sang on, a great chorus of voices offering exaltations on high."

Later, during a generalized discussion of fortified castle keeps, I brought forward the 1:32-scale model, which I carefully showed around, in order to point out salient features of bastille design.

And when we got to the rack—when we got to the rack, I *knew*, before the familiar queries had barely flown from those six-, seven-, and eight-year-old mouths—I *knew* the very questions the students would ask:

"Did the torturers leave the people on that thing for a long time?"

"Did you get taller?"

"Could you get torn in half?"

"One at a time," I implored, raising in the air a steady if scarred hand. I wanted to savor the moment. Those upturned faces before me seemed the faces of angels; pure and spirited, they radiated light. It's a light every teacher lives to bathe in: the luster of the young soul.

"Mr. Robinson?"

It was Sarah. She was sitting in her chair, forsaken. She seemed so far away. Her head was turned to face her peers, and her eyes were full of longing.

"Yeah, Sarah?"

"I think I'm ready to join the class now."

"Are you?"

"I think."

"And what makes you think you're prepared to come back and be one of us?"

All eyes regarded her. We waited. It was a tense moment before Sarah, whispering, explained, "It's dark here. I don't like it."

What we were witnessing was nothing less than a practical demonstration of the plight of the pariah. I took the opportunity for a brief discussion of caste, class, and the thorny social problems surrounding taboo violation and the exclusion and/or integration of individuals and groups according to religion, ethnicity, and "lifestyle."

After which Susy raised her hand and suggested, from the front row, "Make her prove she's ready!"

She was so excited, she inadvertently (or so it seemed) struck her brother in the side of head with her elbow. Brad screamed, pitched forward from his seat, and collapsed to the floor. Susy gazed coolly down at her brother and said, "Stop crying, baby."

And to me, she explained, "He pulls this all the time at home, Mr. Robinson."

I wasn't sure. There are widely ranging schools of thought concerning children who act out dramas of suffering. Do you hasten to their aid? Or do you leave them to sort themselves out, dignify them with the autonomy necessary for growth and individuation? I elected to follow the boy's sister's lead. Fortunately, the distressing noises of Brad were soon drowned by hearty cries from the Harris twins: "Let's see if Sarah's ready to be one of us!"

Up went a chant: "See if she's ready. See if she's ready. See if she's ready. See if she's ready."

It was like a pep rally, or a political convention: total group dynamics, increasing frenzy, catcalls from the ranks of the class. Even overweight Steven got caught up in the excitement of the moment, stamping his feet and motioning with a fist in the air. In the back of the class David, the better to wave his own arms, plunked his infant brother belly-up on the leather edge of their trunk.

Then Susy was on her feet, standing tall before her classmates. Light from the overhead bulb made a shining halo of her hair. And down at her feet: her brother, one hand holding his head, the other reaching out to touch the hem of his sister's dress.

Susy waited for the ruckus to die down. She rested her gaze on Sarah. And said, simply, "The rack."

Well.

I'll admit I was feeling less than one hundred percent that Monday morning. There were, for instance, those sprouting purple welts; no telling the effect, on the brain, of these venomous blemishes. I'd gone without sleep, and it's a sure bet I was running a fever, even a considerable one. Should I have seen it coming, that inaugural—and, as it turned out, final—session of the Pete Robinson Institute, when all the kids (injured Brad excepted; he continued to worm around on the floor, like a hurt animal) turned to see what I would do?

Likewise, how much responsibility must I bear, for what eventually, inevitably occurred, simply because I suggested using the flat, hard surface of a leather-decorated steamer trunk, and Matt and Larry Harris's strong young arms and backs, in lieu of a real rack?

"Go ahead, boys," I said. They didn't need to be told twice. Matt and Larry dove on Sarah like football tackles. Sarah let out a series of impressive screams truly painful to the ear. Finally one of the boys got wise and stripped off his shirt (a "rugby" stretch-knit pullover) and stuffed it in her mouth. "Way to go, Matt. Way to go, Larry," cheered Susy, obviously suffering a wicked crush on one or both of the twins. Other voices shouted more specific encouragements. David, who seemed to appreciate the symmetry between the shirt in Sarah's mouth and the latex pacifier he'd used earlier on Tim, side-coached, "Pick her up. Get her off her feet."

Get her off her feet they did. They hauled Sarah like plunder to David and Tim's trunk. (It was closest.) "Get the baby off there," a Harris shouted. No one wanted to touch Tim. He'd wet himself. It fell to David to scoop him up and carry him, wailing, back to the furnace for another changing. Meanwhile Matt and Larry drop-loaded Sarah onto the trunk. She kicked like a genuine victim of oppression, and it took many hands to restrain her. It was something to see. And to hear, too, when the wadded-up shirt fell from Sarah's mouth, and her shrieking began again, as, from upstairs, the clamor of Meredith's entreaties poured down upon us: "Pete! What's going on down there? Is everything okay? Open this door! What's happening down there? Pete?"

"Ignore that," I instructed the students.

And to my wife: "Hey, stop bothering us. We're trying to do some in-class playacting down here. We're doing an Improvised Creative Activity!"

Eventually the twins managed to get Sarah's mouth replugged. This was a good thing, because Jane was presenting symptoms of really grave nervousness, fretting and trembling. I reminded Jane of her humiliation by Sarah, at the outset of class, for having a straggly little pathetic twig as a toy. This only seemed to confuse her. I still clutched the curled, dripping plumber's snake in my hand; now I offered it to the maudlin girl. "You'll feel better once you get involved in some activities with your friends."

"Mr. Robinson?"

"Yes, Jane?"

"Didn't you say something about people who would kneel down and pray for the people who were getting persecuted?"

"That's right, Jane. The prayers of the faithful accompany the souls of martyrs to the gates of heaven."

"That's what I want to do."

"Pray?"

"Uh-huh."

"Fine. Why don't you do that."

She did. She retreated to a quiet corner and knelt bare-kneed on the floor and raised her hands in the customary palms-together-before-the-breast posture of pious devotion. "Dear Lord, I am praying for the soul of our classmate Sarah who isn't the nicest person in the world. In fact she's stuck up. But she's still a person."

Back at the trunk/rack the Harrises had arranged themselves at either end of Sarah. One Harris struggled with Sarah's bicycle-kicking feet, while the other, the bare-chested twin, yanked more or less viciously on her arms, arms that were thrashing about her head—or, if not thrashing exactly, certainly would've been if only Sarah'd had the strength to liberate her wrists from the boy's grip. "Be still," Susy commanded as the Harrises stretched away, building a rhythm. Gasping sounds escaped Sarah. Her face, with the wet knit shirt spilling about mouth and chin, was a mask of wildness. I noticed Steven backing away from the scene. He watched as if hypnotized, from a distance—like a reticent voyeur fixed on an accident site.

I, too, kept my distance from the low black trunk where Sarah resisted and turned blue.

"Do you hear me?" Susy said over and over again to the gagged girl. "Be still."

It was then I noticed the water coming through the rusted drain grating in the middle of the basement. A tide of brackish backwash was rippling in, seeping in slow estuaries onto the unpainted concrete floor, pooling there and rising like suddenly surfacing groundwater to immerse the padded feet and straggly stomach hairs, and the black tip of the nose of the stuffed bison. It was as if the bison had waded into a watering hole for a cooling drink. Often, during a heavy rain, the basement will flood. Was it raining now? There was no way, down here, of knowing. For a variety of reasons—it being our mascot not least among them—this wetting of the bison was dismaying to me. But due to its location (directly adjacent to the trunk where one of the great—in my opinion—dramas of our culture was currently being enacted, in microcosm), I felt it best to leave it. Let things take care of themselves. The Harrises certainly didn't appear in any mood to welcome interruption, they were working hard. The bare-chested boy, in particular, showed impressive upper-body muscle development for a pre-teen. Must've been all that bow shooting. Hypertrophied lats and ripped abdominals, with minimal subcutaneous fat around the belly, and biceps that sported a handsome blue vein when he closed his hands tightly over Sarah's, breathed in deeply, braced his sneakered feet (splashing, now, in the rapidly expanding lake of drain water), and pulled hard to the cadenced call of Susy's voice, like a sculling captain's, encouraging, "Pull. Pull. Pull. Pull. Pull. Pull. Pull." Pull the boys did, repeatedly, vigorously, splendidly, as, from the shadows nearby, the small voice of Jane proffered blessings: "Dear God, please let Sarah sit with you in the bright blue where all the dead people go who were good when they were alive, because even though Sarah wasn't what you'd call good she wasn't exactly a murderer, she was a kid like me." And so on. The basement air was rank with smells of boys' sweat and Sarah's fear and Tim's soiled diapers. The Harris twins looked huge. The one clutching Sarah's ankles had a moment of difficulty holding on, due to Sarah's schnauzer-faced lace-ups, locked tight in his grip but slipping off her stockinged feet, causing him to pitch suddenly backward and almost lose his balance. But not quite. He was a natural athlete. He snatched the oxfords from Sarah's feet—keeping a firm grip, all the while, on one or the other of her pale thrashing legs—and tossed them furiously away, one shoe spiraling high to crash like a rocket into the basement door, the other speeding heel over toe in the direction of Jane, who, fortunately, saw it flying toward her head and ducked. Now from above came another round of insistent cries from Meredith ("What was *that*? Open this door!"), accompanied by the hysterical metallic rattling of the doorknob against the bolt, and fists or something weightier—Meredith's body?—slamming that sturdy old wooden door, sending audible and sub-audible concussions rumbling thunderously over our heads. Yet it was as if those detonations occurred somewhere far away. Not one among us, neither David nor Tim, nor Steven nor Jane, nor even little Brad, moved. (Brad did, however, clutch his head, which was bleeding; it would subsequently be revealed that the child suffered partial sight loss damage from sister Susy's lacerating elbow, though at the time who could know this?) We were busy watching the terrible cleaving of Sarah; listening to Susy's shrill trumpeting, the twins' virile grunting, and to new and stranger sounds arising from the elongate form of Sarah's body stretched like pink corpulent matter across a grimy storage trunk, her innocent bloodless face rag-stuffed and screaming silent screams at the ceiling while shoulder and hip and wrist and ankle bones pitched and rocked and pivoted grotesquely before at last tumbling free from their sockets as the grim separation took place at the soft center of her, the tearing of Sarah's muscle and cartilage and bone.

Or perhaps it was only the basement door coming off its hinges, that made that awful cracking.

Looking back on it all, now—on the exploding door and Sarah's simultaneous final, convulsive spasms; on the other children wading agitatedly in deepening greasy drain water rising to stain Sarah's twisted appendages hanging limply from the calfskin and brass gilt edges of the trunk; on the sensational entrance of Meredith, swooping augustly down the stairs with Hope fastened like a crazed baby marsupial to her breast, stopping momentarily to gaze around, to take in that dismal scene, before splashing across the channel of basement floodwater to kneel at Sarah's side, to gather, for some unclear reason, in her hands, a clump of the girl's sodden hair—she peered up at me then, my beautiful, terrified wife, one hand clutching Sarah's hair, the other still cradling Hope, and her mouth, my wife's mouth, slowly opening to form the words "Murderer, Murderer"—looking back on all this, now, from the relative safety of my padlocked attic, I can only confess that I am sorry.

Nowadays, the profession of teacher is little valued. Who will steward the coming generations? Who will teach the bitter examples of history?

As always, I believe in primary education and the betterment of our fallen world through the intercession of children. Down comes the rain. It is afternoon. Who knows what day. The ball-strewn tennis courts are abandoned and the sky is howling black. My desk remains piled with things to do; in a minute I'll get busy. I miss my wife awfully.

Lightning flashes over the sea. A few seconds later thunder sounds. Or maybe it's just one of the leftover mines going off in the wretched recesses of the park. Nothing moves there except the tops of trees bowing beneath rain, windblown in sheets that split open over the roofs of houses, spilling down trellises and window casements, draining away into yards and gardens, over sidewalks, doorsteps, and drives: the seeping, luminescent world. It's not good to go outside. There are snakes. And the violet welts covering my hands and arms, far from receding, have steadily flourished, discoloring the skin and filling my mind with feverish convictions. Sweat and dementia. At night, sleepless and alone, I become certain of death. Each day, the water in the basement rises a tiny bit higher. On its surface float books, toys and dolls, flower petals, a diaper. You don't want to go down there. The kitchen's a mess. The power is out. There's a smell of rot. Rotten lungs, rotten genitals, rotten heart. Why can't we all be happy with what we're given in life? For my part, I can only hope that the unfortunate incident involving my sweet young pupil will not prejudice my constituency in the upcoming general elections. Compassion is everything. As for poor Sarah, suffice it to say she had to be carried out of there. Things are bad all over. Nothing looks promising. I wish Meredith would come home. I want to fuck her. She does not think well of me.